MW00795910

THE HERO SHE DESERVES

UNBROKEN HEROES
BOOK 4

ANNA HACKETT

The Hero She Deserves

Published by Anna Hackett

Copyright 2024 by Anna Hackett

Cover by Hang Le Designs

Cover image by Wander Aguiar

Edits by Tanya Saari

ISBN (ebook): 978-1-923134-44-7

ISBN (paperback): 978-1-923134-45-4

This book is a work of fiction. All names, characters, places and
incidents are either the product of the author's imagination or are used
fictitiously. Any resemblance to actual persons, events or places is
coincidental. No part of this book may be reproduced, scanned, or
distributed in any printed or electronic form.

WHAT READERS ARE SAYING ABOUT ANNA'S ACTION ROMANCE

The Powerbroker - Romantic Book of the Year (Ruby) winner 2022

Heart of Eon - Romantic Book of the Year (Ruby) winner 2020

Cyborg - PRISM Award Winner 2019

Unfathomed and Unmapped - Romantic Book of the Year (Ruby) finalists 2018

Unexplored – Romantic Book of the Year (Ruby) Novella Winner 2017

Return to Dark Earth – One of Library Journal's Best E-Original Books for 2015 and two-time SFR Galaxy Awards winner

At Star's End – One of Library Journal's Best E-Original Romances for 2014

The Phoenix Adventures – SFR Galaxy Award Winner for Most Fun New Series and "Why Isn't This a Movie?" Series

Beneath a Trojan Moon – SFR Galaxy Award Winner and RWAus Ella Award Winner

Hell Squad – SFR Galaxy Award for best Post-Apocalypse for Readers who don't like Post-Apocalypse

"Like Indiana Jones meets Star Wars. A treasure hunt with a steamy romance." – SFF Dragon, review of *Among Galactic Ruins*

"Action, danger, aliens, romance – yup, it's another great book from Anna Hackett!" – Book Gannet Reviews, review of *Hell Squad: Marcus*

Sign up for my VIP mailing list and get your *free box set* containing three action-packed romances.

Visit here to get started: www.annahackett.com

CHAPTER ONE

Deputy Sheriff Sawyer Lane shoved out of his sheriff's department SUV and headed for his place.

Thank God this day was over. Most of the time, being a deputy sheriff on Maui suited him. Usually, he dealt with petty theft and lost tourists. *Easy.* There was no one shooting at him. No friends dying.

He stopped at the base of the steps to his front porch and rubbed the back of his stiff neck. Today was the exception to that rule. There had been a bad car accident on the Kahekili Highway. Two carloads of tourists had hit each other. An eight-year-old boy had been trapped in the twisted metal. Sawyer had held the boy's hand, trying to keep him calm, while the firefighters had cut him free.

Hell, he hoped the kid made it. The boy had been airlifted to the Maui Medical Center, and his prognosis had been good. Sawyer would call into the center in the morning and see how Tyler was doing.

His boots clunked on the wooden steps, and he

pulled out his keys and unlocked the front door. He wanted a beer, and a few moments of solitude. He slowed on his walk to the kitchen, and stared out the window above the sink. Looking at the ocean never failed to soothe him. Just looking at the water evened out the ragged edges inside.

Sawyer knew that moving to Hawaii after he'd left the military had saved his life.

The memories tugged at him—both good and bad. Sometimes he missed his team, missed the importance of the work. Most of the time, he didn't. Especially at night when he couldn't sleep.

He couldn't remember the last time he'd had a full night's sleep.

He pulled open the fridge and grabbed a bottle of Black Pearl made right there on Maui by the Maui Brewing Company. He popped the top and had just lifted the bottle to his lips when his cellphone rang.

"Dammit." Setting the bottle down, he pulled his phone out and saw Benny's name on the screen. "Lane."

"Bro, you know it's me, why do you always answer with your surname?"

"It's how I answer the phone." Despite the bro, Benny was Sawyer's cousin. Somehow, despite being born and raised in Montana, Benny had fallen in love with the ocean. He had long, sun-bleached hair, and was a champion windsurfer. He'd come to Paia, on Maui's north shore, as it was the windsurfing capital of Hawaii. He'd then fallen in love with a local Hawaiian woman.

"You home?" Benny asked.

"Yeah, I just stepped inside."

"Sawyer, man, I need a favor."

Sawyer sighed. His hope of a beer and solitude evaporating. "Go on."

"Uncle Duke called and said the smoke alarm is going off at Archer's place."

Sawyer's gaze moved to the window again. Down closer to the water he saw the roof of Archer Kent's holiday home. It was perched right on the water's edge and fancy as hell. It was nothing like Sawyer's simple, traditional, wooden cottage.

Archer only used the place a couple of times a year and was rarely there. He and Benny were friends from their early windsurfing days. Archer had gone on to become a successful stuntman, and lived in LA.

Sawyer frowned. "I don't see any smoke."

"Can you check it out? Uncle Duke was walking past and heard the noise. I'd drive over, but Kalani just got in the shower. We're going to her parents' place for dinner. Some of her aunts and uncles are over from the Big Island."

Sawyer knew exactly how big Benny's wife's family was. They'd welcomed Benny with open arms, then when his cousin had convinced Sawyer to come and stay, they'd welcomed him, too.

Benny was on the other side of town. If he came over to check, he'd be late for his family dinner. "It's fine. I'll go over and take a look."

"Bro, I owe you. Thanks."

"Say hi to Kalani, and I'll see you later."

Relaxing with his Black Pearl would have to wait.

He didn't bother driving, and instead, took the

winding path through the trees. Flowers were blooming somewhere, scenting the air. This path led down to the beach, and he often went down to jog on the sand when he had the time.

Archer's place came into view. It definitely made Sawyer's simple cottage look bland and boring. It was modern, with lots of glass, wood, and steel. As he neared the front door, the insistent beep of a smoke alarm became audible.

He also noted a rental car out front. A flashy, little BMW.

He frowned. Had someone broken in? As far as he knew, Archer wasn't planning a visit any time soon.

He knocked on the front door. "Sheriff's Department."

There was no response. He suspected if there was someone here, they couldn't hear him over the racket of the smoke alarm. He tried the door handle, and it opened. He entered and briefly touched the gun holster on his hip. There was no smoke at least.

"Sheriff's Department." He walked through to the sleek living area. Hell, it sure was something, with a shiny, marble-tile floor and furniture with clean, modern lines. He had a perfect view of the glittering pool, and the ocean beyond. He turned into the kitchen, and the smell of smoke hit him.

He took another step, then his brain sort of short-circuited.

The first thing he saw was sleek, smooth legs.

The woman was standing on a chair, wrapped in a towel, and reaching for the blaring alarm. The towel barely covered what Sawyer assumed was a very naked body. Her long, dark hair was wet and falling over her smooth shoulders in a loose mess, so he guessed she'd just come out of the shower. His gaze drifted lower. Her toenails were painted red.

He cleared his throat, attempting to get her attention, and let his brain cells start firing again. She didn't hear him.

"You damn, annoying, crazy-inducing—" She went up on her toes.

The towel rose another inch, barely covering anything.

He took a step closer. Her head whipped up, and brilliant-blue eyes went wide.

And for the first time in his life, Sawyer forgot his own name.

She had a beautiful, oval-shaped face, with pale, creamy skin, and perfect lips. Her hair wasn't brown as he'd first thought, but a deep red.

And he realized he'd seen it before.

She let out a squeak and lost her balance.

Sawyer lunged forward and caught her before she hit the floor. She landed in his arms.

"Oh, my God." She pressed a hand against his chest.

He set her on her feet, and she scrambled away from him. The towel slipped and with a gasp, she grabbed for it.

Too late.

The towel slithered to the floor, leaving Hollis Stanton—Hollywood's hottest, Oscar-winning actress —naked.

5

HOLLIS FROZE.

Oh, God. Thoughts ran through her head, lightning fast. The smoke alarm was ringing painfully in her ears. She was naked—something she usually got paid a lot of money for. And there was a strange man in her house.

Added to all that, her coffee machine was on fire.

The man stepped closer and picked up the towel.

Oh... She snatched the towel and wrapped it around herself. Her throat tightened. Why was this guy in her house? Was he going to hurt her?

Swallowing, she met the man's gaze. He was staring at her with a kind of entranced look on his face. Then he shook his head, like he was waking himself up.

"Sheriff's Department, ma'am."

Sheriff? Hollis blinked, and that's when she realized he was wearing a uniform—khaki shirt and dark green pants. *Oh, sheriff.* Relief punched through her. The tan shirt was stretched tight over massive shoulders, a broad chest, and muscular arms.

Wow. Hawaii knew how to make their sheriffs.

The sheriff didn't need the chair. He reached up, and with a ripple of muscles, turned off the smoke alarm.

Blessed silence fell. *Hallelujah.* Her ears were still ringing, though.

The sheriff stepped past her and eyed the smoking ruin of her coffee machine.

"Um, I'm not sure what happened. I started the machine and went to take a shower." She waved at the small fire extinguisher she'd found under the sink. "I used that, but I think the coffee machine is dead."

He lifted the fire extinguisher, and she watched him carefully spray the smoking coffee machine again.

She blinked. He looked so...competent and in charge.

She'd worked alongside actors who'd portrayed cops, soldiers, and heroes. They always seemed so fake.

Not this man.

"It's definitely dead." His voice was a low rumble. He leaned over to set the fire extinguisher down, and her gaze went to the most muscular ass she'd ever seen—and she'd seen quite a few in Hollywood.

Then he turned to face her.

Rugged. There was no other word to describe that face. Well, maybe solid, masculine. She'd heard actors called rugged, but they didn't hold a candle to this guy. The beard—something more than scruff but less than full lumberjack—just added to the rugged vibe.

"Thank you." She tucked the towel a little more securely around her body and tried *not* to focus on the fact that she'd just been completely naked in front of this man. "I didn't mean to start a fire." She glanced at the black ruin and winced.

"I'm Deputy Sheriff Sawyer Lane. You're a friend of Archer Kent?"

That deep voice shivered through her. She stared at him and realized he was waiting for a response.

Right, he'd asked her a question. She shoved a hand through her wet hair. "Yes. Archer is letting me stay here for a bit."

That direct hazel gaze hit her—his eyes were mostly

green, but with a few flecks of gold. She felt like his gaze could see inside her, see all her secrets.

Hollis had been an actress since her teens. She'd gotten very good at never giving her secrets away... because they'd likely end up in a tabloid.

She lifted her chin. "I'm...Holli. Thank you, Sheriff."

"Deputy." He eyed her. "You staying long, Holli?"

There was no sign of recognition on his face. She wasn't surprised since she was wet, makeup free, and only wearing a towel.

"I'm not sure yet. I'm taking a...break."

She wished it was that simple. She was trying to escape from the fact that she was either in danger or losing her mind. She wasn't sure which one she'd prefer at this stage.

She straightened. "Well, thank you again for silencing the alarm."

Deputy Sheriff Sawyer Lane nodded, then strode past her. She caught his scent—some woodsy cologne that gave her an image of him chopping wood.

Jeez, imagination, we're on Maui. He's not a lumberjack.

Near the front door, the deputy paused.

"Ma'am, if you want coffee, there's a good place in Paia. It's called Island Brew."

She nodded. "Thanks. I don't really function without a decent caffeine hit."

"They'll definitely be able to provide that." He gave her a chin lift.

As he closed the door behind him, heat filled her cheeks. Hollis pressed her palms over them.

Way to go, Hollis. You burned down your coffee machine and flashed the local deputy.

She lifted her chin. Hell, she was no stranger to some embarrassment and humiliation. Being an actor, you frequently had to deal with bad reviews, critics, and Internet trolls.

She'd probably never see Deputy Hottie again, anyway. She was here to lie low.

A cold shiver ran down her spine.

She needed to finish her shower and attempt to cook some dinner with the groceries she'd bought after she'd landed. Hopefully she could manage that without burning the house down.

CHAPTER TWO

She woke up, heart pounding.

Hollis sat up. The bed was a mess and her eyes were gritty. She hadn't slept well thanks to the nightmares. She hadn't slept well since this entire situation had started. She pushed her tangled hair back and sighed.

Another day powered by coffee.

Except that the coffee machine was a burnt husk that she'd dragged outside and dumped in the trash.

Groaning, she dropped her head in her hands, trying to shake off the night spent staring at the ceiling, dreaming of shadowy figures, hearing noises, and worrying that someone was going to break in.

No one's going to break in, Hols. No one knows you're in Hawaii.

She rose and opened the curtains.

"Oh." The beautiful ocean water sparkled a brilliant blue. She felt some of the tension drain away as she soaked in the view.

She was far away from the person who was tormenting her.

She knew who was behind it.

Michael Reuben—eccentric and powerful movie producer. She'd gone to a party at his Hollywood mansion. One, she wanted it noted that she didn't even want to go. No, her agent had talked her into it. She still hadn't quite forgiven Tavion for it.

While she'd been looking for the bathroom in the huge, sprawling house—and counting down the minutes until she could leave—she'd gotten lost. She'd heard Reuben's voice down the hall and overheard him talking to someone. She'd only picked up a few words about shipments and sanctions. Then he and whoever he was talking with had spoken in Russian.

As far as she knew, Reuben wasn't Russian.

She'd tried to sneak off, but one of Reuben's bodyguards had spotted her. A creepy guy with a scar on his cheek and a knife, of all things, on his belt. She'd flashed him an Oscar-worthy smile.

"I'm so lost. I'm looking for the ladies' room." She added a little hiccup and a tipsy grin for effect. Drunk woman, nothing to worry about.

Scarface scowled at her, then Reuben stepped out of his office. In his sixties, he was of medium height, with a rotund middle, and a long, hawkish nose. He always wore a suit.

"Oh, Michael, I didn't know you were up here," she said. "Why aren't you at the party?"

"I'm returning now." He shot her a hard stare.

Full of nerves, it had taken all the acting skills Hollis possessed to keep her smile in place.

"The bathroom is down the next hall," Reuben said. "On the left."

"Thank you." She gave a breezy wave and turned.

In the bathroom, she'd felt sick. She knew she'd heard something she shouldn't have. Shipments of what? And if they were going to or from Russia, it had to be something very illegal. She knew there were so many sanctions on the country right now.

Hollis had tried to blow it off and forget.

But after that night, things had started happening. She was sure she was being watched, and a few times, she was certain she'd been followed.

That wasn't uncommon for her. The paparazzi were a constant pest, but this had felt different.

Every now and then, she'd catch a glimpse of a shadow or a silhouette, but then, nothing. Some days, she was worried that she was losing her mind.

She'd considered going to the police, but to tell them what? Hearing a few words, and thinking she was being followed weren't really evidence of anything.

She'd considered hiring a full-time bodyguard. She usually only had security and bodyguards during the frenzy of a movie opening. Normally, she trusted that her home security system was enough.

Then someone had crashed into her car.

Apart from some whiplash, thankfully, she'd been uninjured. The big, black SUV that had hit her had no plates, and the driver had driven off without checking on her.

She gripped the curtains, staring out at the beach. The worst thing was finding a secret camera in her house. In her bedroom.

Someone had been in her home.

That's when she'd finally told her agent what was happening.

Tavion had lost his mind and helped her run.

Archer, who was also a client of Tave's had offered to loan her his house on Maui. She'd traveled to San Diego, then Tave had hired a private jet in Archer's name so there was no record of her arriving in Hawaii.

"You're safe," she whispered.

She had to hope that this situation would blow over. If Reuben was really concerned that she'd heard something, and she did nothing, and his mysterious shipments arrived, then surely he'd leave her alone.

What if he was doing something really illegal?

She rubbed her temple. She wasn't law enforcement. For all she knew, he was smuggling caviar. Wait and see. It wasn't much of a plan, but it was the best she had. She had no real proof of anything. Sometimes, she was worried she was imagining it all and losing her mind.

You're in paradise, Hols. Relax.

She was a little burned out. She'd done four big films in the last two years. That meant long hours rehearsing and filming, not to mention all the press tours to promote the films. Then this situation.

It was no wonder she was running on nerves.

She straightened her shoulders. Right now, the only thing she was going to worry about was getting some caffeine.

She pulled on leggings and a T-shirt, then tucked her hair under a blue ball cap. To finish it off, she slid on some huge sunglasses.

She never wore ball caps, so hopefully no one recognized her. It was unlikely she could stay incognito forever, but thankfully, Paia was small and wasn't quite as touristy as some of Maui's other destinations.

In her rental car, she tapped Island Brew into the navigation system. Of course, that made her think of Deputy Hottie. She shivered. She wished she'd spent the night dreaming of him instead of being hunted by faceless bad guys.

With a shake of her head, she set off down the road. As lush trees gave way to the town, she smiled. Paia had a funky, 6os, California-beach-town vibe. There were quaint shops and restaurants, and most of the buildings were painted in pastel colors.

She spotted Island Brew—it was a pale-blue building with white trim. She found a parking spot out front. The logo on the building had a coffee mug with a shell on the front, and a curl of steam rising from the top.

Before she got out of the car, her cellphone rang. It was Tave.

"Hey, you," she said.

"You okay?" he asked in his smooth, deep voice.

If there was ever a man with the voice for radio or voice overs, it was Tavion Hall. Instead, he'd become an agent to the stars. He was one of the most sought-after agents in Hollywood.

"I'm in the most beautiful spot in the world."

"That's not what I asked, Hols."

Tave wasn't just her agent, he was also a friend. To be honest, she didn't have too many true friends. The downside of fame was that you ended up with fans and acquaintances, but not a lot of true, deep connections.

Hell, she'd never had many true, deep connections anyway. She was coming to suspect she just wasn't wired for them.

She stared blindly through the windshield and sighed. "I'm okay. Not sleeping well, but I'm better now I'm out of LA. Except I set Archer's coffee machine on fire."

Tave made a sound.

She knew that sound. He was unhappy. She could picture him sitting at his glossy black desk in his office in Beverly Hills. He'd be wearing tailored pants that hugged his lean form and a white shirt that looked amazing with his dark skin. Tavion always looked polished and stylish.

"I'll be okay, Tave. I just got here. Give me some time."

"All right, Red. You want me to come out there?"

Her chest twanged. Coming from Tave, who thought LA was the center of the universe, it was big. "I know how busy you are. You don't need to come and hold my hand."

"Never too busy for you. And you never want anyone to hold your hand, but sometimes, Red, it's okay to hold on."

"I'll be fine." Because she was always fine. She'd made her life exactly what she wanted, on her own, without anyone helping her.

He sighed. "If anything worries you, then you call me."

"I will. You'll be happy to hear that I met a member of local law enforcement."

"Really? You get another speeding ticket?"

"Ha ha. I only got that *one* ticket. I'm not a speed demon."

"It was three."

"Fine. But no, I met Deputy Hottie because I set the coffee machine on fire, and my smoke alarm was going off and I couldn't silence the damn thing. He came to my rescue."

"Deputy Hottie, huh?"

"Big, muscular, and rugged. Looks a little like the actor from the *Reacher* TV show."

Tave made another sound. This one appreciative. "Maybe I do need to come and visit."

"I don't think he swings your way. Anyway, I'm at the local coffee shop wearing a god-awful ball cap and hoping I can get a coffee without anyone recognizing me."

"Okay, Red, go get your caffeine. Enjoy paradise and I'll check in soon."

"Bye, Tave."

"Stay safe, Hols."

After tucking her phone away, Hollis headed into Island Brew. As she opened the door, the sweet scent of coffee hit her. She breathed it deep. *Come to mama.*

The place was busy—with a mix of mostly locals and a couple of tourists. An eclectic mix of tables were scattered around, all topped with shell-shaped sugar holders. A young man and woman stood behind the counter, blue aprons tied around their waists, working in tandem. From the looks of their dark hair and eyes, and brown skin, they were local Hawaiians. She guessed they were in their late twenties. The man was short and wide, and the woman was a little taller and curvy.

Hollis waited until most of the crowd had cleared. As she approached, the woman saw Hollis and gasped. "Oh my God."

Hollis froze. Oh no, someone had recognized her already.

"I *love* those sunglasses," the woman exclaimed. "Where are they from? I need a pair."

The man snorted. "Sis, you have like a hundred pairs."

"I'm always searching for the right ones. *Those* are the right ones."

"Um...they're from a little store in—" she almost said LA "—San Diego."

The woman's face fell. "The mainland? That's too far away."

"I'll say," the man added. "You've never been to the mainland."

"Nor have you." The woman shrugged. "We live in the most perfect place in the world, so why would I go to the mainland?"

Hollis couldn't argue with that.

"What would you like?" The man smiled. "I'm Koa, and this is my twin sister, Kiana. This is our place."

"I need a coffee, like yesterday," Hollis said. "There was an unfortunate incident with my coffee machine. Can I get a latte?"

Kiana's dark eyes narrowed. She looked like a scientist, and Hollis was her experiment.

"You need a special latte." The woman crossed her arms and tapped a finger against her chin. "I'll customize one for you."

"You will?"

"It's my thing."

Beside her, Koa nodded. "It is. She's a coffee maestro."

"Okay," Hollis replied.

Kiana studied her some more. "A vanilla coconut latte." She turned to the large coffee machine.

"Ooh," Koa said.

Hollis kept her smile in place and prayed the twins didn't ruin her caffeine hit.

"Are you hiding a black eye under those glasses?" Koa asked.

"Um, no."

"Then why are you wearing them inside?"

"Because I'm eccentric like that."

He cocked his head. "You famous, or something?"

Her stomach tangled in knots. "Or something."

Koa shrugged. "We don't care."

"Let the woman sit down, Koa," Kiana groused.

Hollis paid, then Kiana set a coffee down on the counter. It was frothy on top with a swirl in the center. The swirl was a dolphin. Hollis laughed. "Oh, that is so cute. And you're so talented."

Kiana smiled.

"It looks great." Hollis lifted the mug cautiously and

sipped. She felt them watching her. Then her eyes popped wide. "Oh my God, this is *delicious*."

Kiana beamed, then high-fived her brother.

"You did it again, sis." Koa turned to Hollis. "Sit, pretty tourist with the sunglasses. I'm bringing you a coconut cookie to go with your latte. Dad made them, and he is a guru in the kitchen."

"Okay." Hollis turned and ran into a wall.

It took her a second to realize it wasn't a wall, but a hard chest. A massive, muscled chest covered in khaki.

Quick as she could, she moved her mug up, trying not to spill the coffee, but a little slosh of froth landed on Sawyer Lane's beard-covered jaw.

She looked up into piercing hazel eyes.

———

"SORRY. *SO* SORRY."

Hollis Stanton swiped elegant fingers over his chin.

"It's pure luck that I didn't get any on your shirt."

Her red hair was tucked away under a hat, and huge sunglasses dominated her face. He guessed it would fool someone at a glance.

Sawyer watched her lick her fingers and his cock took a hell of a lot of notice.

Damn. The last thing he needed was an attraction to an actress. His cock had been practically asleep since he'd left the military. He'd been fine with that. Now was not the time for it to wake up and cause problems.

"I wasn't watching where I was going," she said. "Sorry."

She was stunning, even with the ridiculous, oversized glasses perched on her nose. All he could see was porcelain skin, and lush lips. She wasn't cookie-cutter pretty like a lot of the young actresses he saw on the screen. She had her own look, and it made her unique.

"You tried Island Brew," he said.

She smiled. "I was in dire need of caffeine."

He leaned in. "Then you shouldn't have set your coffee machine on fire."

"That was an accident."

"Hey there, Sawyer." Koa bustled over, holding up a large takeout cup. "Giant Americano, with a touch of caramel."

"Thanks, Koa. Put it on my tab."

"Done." The man's interested gaze moved from Sawyer to Hollis, then back to Sawyer. "You sit too, Sawyer. Join our lovely guest here." He practically shoved Hollis into a seat at a small table. Then he gave Sawyer a shove.

Sawyer didn't move.

"Kiana's bringing cookies out for the both of you."

"Your dad make them?" Sawyer asked.

"Does the sun rise in the east?"

He knew he shouldn't sit. He shouldn't get anywhere near Hollis Stanton. He needed to drive over to Kahului and get to work. Paia was small but thankfully only a fifteen-minute drive from the airport and the largest town on the island. That's where the sherrif's department office was.

He sat.

Hollis sipped her coffee and gave a quiet moan.

Dammit. He shifted in his chair, his cock hardening further. Did she moan like that when she was turned on?

No. No thoughts like that.

"So, you're on a break from filming?" he asked.

She froze and looked up. "You know who I am."

"Well, you definitely weren't wearing any disguises yesterday."

A blush filled her cheeks.

He wouldn't guess an experienced actress would blush. It was pretty. "And I am a deputy sheriff. We're observant."

"I'm taking a little vacation."

"Coconut cookies." Koa set a plate down. "Enjoy."

Hollis glanced at him and smiled. Then she threw a cautious gaze around the cafe.

Sawyer leaned in. "I'm not planning to tell anyone who you are."

Relief covered her face. "Thank you, Deputy...Lane, right?"

"It's Sawyer." *Shit.* He shouldn't have said that.

She smiled, and it hit him in the gut. He'd seen it on screen, but in real life, it was even better.

"And I'm Hollis."

"Not Holli?"

"That's just my undercover name. I don't think I look like a Holli."

He nodded. "Hollis suits you better."

"It was my grandmother's maiden name. My brother was Cavendish, so I think I got the better deal."

"Agreed." He noted the *was*, but didn't pry.

She leaned her elbows on the table. "Are you from Hawaii, Sawyer?"

"No. I've been here almost a year. I'm from Montana originally."

"You're a long way from home. Were you a cowboy?"

He laughed. "No, my dad worked in construction."

"Your parents still there?"

"No. My dad passed away a few years back, and my mom moved to Florida." He'd bought her a little condo, and she loved it.

"I'm sorry about your dad," Hollis said.

He nodded. "He's been gone a while. Good, salt-of-the-earth man. He was a good dad."

"Sounds like you were lucky to have him." There was a wistful note to her voice.

He studied her closer, but she lifted her coffee and glanced away. "I'm just glad that my mom's happy in Florida. She has good friends."

"No siblings?"

"No. Mom and Dad tried for more, but it didn't work out."

She sipped her coffee. "So how did you end up in Hawaii?"

"I got out of the military and was looking for something different." In reality, he'd been hanging on by a thread. Afraid he was going to lose it. "My cousin is married to a Hawaiian woman. He loves Maui, and convinced me to come."

"And you became a deputy sheriff, and the rest is history?"

"Something like that." He sipped his own coffee. "I like it here."

She looked around the coffee shop. "I bet it's different from military life."

"Definitely." He glanced around, checking that no one was close by. "How did you get into acting?"

"*Annie.*"

He raised a brow.

"The orphan, Annie. I was nine and we went to see it because my brother was working backstage for the production. I was mesmerized. This girl, with red hair—which I took as a sign—was singing and dancing, and being so big and bold. I was hooked."

"And the rest is history."

She rolled her beautiful eyes. "Oh no. I told my mom that I was going to become an actress, and she freaked. Single mom, working two jobs, desperate for some sort of security. She didn't see acting as a good career path, and she wasn't afraid to share her thoughts."

He frowned. "Winning an Oscar must have changed her mind."

She shrugged. "Not really. I think she's still waiting for me to wake up one day and realize I need to be a doctor or lawyer. It's fine. I know I'm doing what I'm supposed to be doing. I love it."

That smile again.

"Good for you."

She lifted her coffee mug. "Thanks."

He checked his watch. "I need to get to work."

"Oh, I'm holding you up. Sorry. Nice chatting with you, Deputy La—"

He raised a brow.

"Sawyer." She grabbed a cookie. "Thanks for the coffee recommendation, too. Oh, and the rescue yesterday."

He rose, feeling strangely reluctant. "Try not to set any more fires today. I'd hate to have to arrest you for being a firebug."

Her laugh went straight to his gut. "I'll try my best."

CHAPTER THREE

B end. Stretch. Breathe.
Hollis held the downward-dog pose, breathing calmly. She was on the beach, doing yoga to relax. The morning sun was warm on her skin, the sand was cool under her feet, and the gentle sounds of the waves lapping on the shore echoed in her ears.

But she didn't feel relaxed.

With a huff, she dropped onto her towel. She was in literal paradise, and she still couldn't relax.

She'd slept badly...again. Dreams of Reuben standing over her, holding a knife, had plagued her. She knew she shouldn't have accepted that role in that horror movie a few months back. It had been a fun cameo, where she'd been brutally murdered in the opening scene. It had only been one day of filming, and it had been lots of fun.

Except, it had left her with perfect mental images of messy stabbings.

"Michael Reuben doesn't know where you are," she whispered. "Just breathe."

She did some deep breathing. Two days in Hawaii, and she was still edgy and tense. She pushed her hair back.

The only time she hadn't been stressed was when she'd been talking with Deputy Hottie.

Sawyer.

Okay, last night in bed with her vibrator she hadn't been stressed, either. She bit her lip. She'd been imagining Sawyer's head between her legs instead of her toy.

Phew, Hollis, enough. You're not here for a holiday fling.

No, she was in hiding until things cooled off, until she could come up with a way to deal with her situation.

Maybe she should shoot a movie far away? Africa? Scandinavia? Antarctica?

Something made her turn her head, and everything inside her stilled. The powerful form of Sawyer Lane was jogging up the beach. He was only wearing black athletic shorts, and no shirt.

Her heart thudded. *Holy hotness.* Her mouth went dry. As he got closer, every line of his chest and abs became visible in perfect detail. A band of black ink circled one large bicep.

God, she'd seen plenty of hard bodies in Hollywood before, but Sawyer was pure muscle, and so real. He wasn't lean and perfect, sculpted by a trainer. These were muscles he used.

Her gaze traced the deep *V* of muscles that disappeared into his running shorts.

He stopped a few feet away, pulling his earbuds out of his ears. "Good morning."

"Morning." Her voice was a little hoarse. *Stop staring, Hols.* "You run every day?"

"No, just when I have the time to get down here. It's my day off today."

She waved at her towel, and he sat down beside her. She got a whiff of soap and male sweat. Her belly coiled.

"What are you doing?" he asked.

"I was trying to do yoga. To relax."

He eyed her. "You don't seem very relaxed."

"I'm not. Yet." She gritted her teeth. "I'm working on it."

He was quiet for a moment. "You need to stop trying."

She turned to look at him. "What?"

"You're overthinking it."

"I'm *really* good at overthinking."

He snorted. "It's like when you're trying to go to sleep, and you're concentrating on it really hard, and it does the opposite."

"Oh, I'm well acquainted with that, too."

"You running from something, Hollis?"

His deep voice shivered through her, and she turned to look at the ocean. "No. I'm just an overworked actress who needs to learn to relax."

He stayed silent.

"I promise," she said. "There are no horrid tabloid exclusives I'm running from, or rumored pregnancies."

His gaze dropped to her belly.

Hollis was really glad she was wearing her cute, mint-green leggings and matching top.

"Jealous boyfriend?" he asked

"No. No boyfriend."

"Crazy stalker?"

She managed to laugh, since that one was a little too close for comfort. "Not this week."

"You got a cellphone?"

"Yes." She grabbed it off the towel.

"I'll give you my number. In case you need anything."

She felt a pulse in her belly. *How about no-holds-barred, hot sex?* She cleared her throat. *Get your mind out of the gutter, Hollis. He's just being nice and friendly. It's his job.*

He rattled off his number and she tapped it in. She saved it as Deputy Hottie, but was careful to tilt the screen away so he couldn't see.

They sat together for a moment in the quiet, and Hollis was surprised at how nice it felt. Back home, everyone was always clamoring to fill the silence. She watched some windsurfers in the distance, zipping across the waves.

"Have you ever windsurfed?" Sawyer asked.

"No."

"My cousin's really good. He's an instructor, if you want to learn."

"Thanks, but no. My agent would have an aneurysm if I did something like windsurfing. Do you windsurf?"

He shrugged one broad shoulder. "I tried it a few times when I first moved here. It's fun, but not for me."

She toyed with the end of the towel. She felt this strange urge to know more about him. "Was it hard for you? Adjusting to life here after the military?"

He was silent so long, she was worried she'd over-stepped.

"Sorry, it's none of my business."

"It was hard. It still is some days, but it gets better over time. Slowly." He rose and dusted the sand off. "Whatever's stressing you out, Hollis, you can change it."

Damn. He'd warned her that he was observant. She wrapped her arms around her legs. "Not every situation is that easy,"

"No, but you can still take action." He stuck his earbuds back in. "If you need anything, just call."

She watched as he jogged away.

Okay, okay, she watched his ass and those thick, muscular thighs as he jogged away. She was only human.

At least she was thinking of something that wasn't her own miserable situation.

SAWYER STARTLED AWAKE, his heart pounding, his chest tight.

"Fuck."

He was in the armchair in his living room. He didn't bother trying to sleep in his bed anymore. It never worked. In the armchair, he usually dozed off and caught some catnaps.

He glanced at his watch and swallowed a curse. It was only 11:30 PM. He'd only been asleep for forty-five minutes. His skin was slick with perspiration. He sat there, breathing hard, as the nightmare slowly faded.

But the screams never quite went away, nor the memory of the flicker of flames.

With another curse, he rose. When he'd fallen asleep, it had been to the pleasant image of Hollis in leggings and a tiny top that hugged her perfect breasts.

But not even that had kept the nightmare at bay.

Grabbing his phone, he padded into the kitchen. He never knew when work might call him in.

He was no stranger to late-night wake-ups. It had been almost eighteen months since he'd left Ghost Ops. To be fair, the last few years on the team hadn't been the same. Not since the best commander he'd ever worked with had left, but Sawyer had stayed on because he knew the team did important work.

Until...

Until he couldn't stay any longer.

He grabbed a beer from the fridge. He didn't care that he was only in his boxer briefs; he walked out onto his deck.

The darkness surrounded him. The cool, night air dried the sweat on his skin. He set his phone on the railing, then leaned against the wood, and sipped.

His gaze moved toward the roof of Hollis's place. He imagined her in bed, red hair everywhere.

He took another sip.

There was a story there. Something was bothering her. Sawyer had a finely tuned sense for trouble, and something was making her afraid.

What would terrify a wealthy, A-list actress, who had it all?

It sounded like her family wasn't tight. It was hard to

picture a mom who wasn't impressed when their kid won an Oscar, and had starred in some of the most popular movies of the last decade.

He stared out toward the ocean. He should be keeping his mind and eyes off her. He had no time for a woman. All the shit he had lurking inside him...he had no desire to inflict that on anyone.

Those long-ago screams echoed in his head again.

He shook his head, and took another sip of beer. At that moment, his phone vibrated with a message.

The screen lit up, and he glanced at it.

You doing okay?

Damn, Vander Norcross—best Ghost Ops commander Sawyer had ever known—was uncanny as fuck. The man could sense stuff no one else would notice.

He tapped back a message.

Another night in paradise.

A second later, his phone rang.

"It's late in San Francisco," Sawyer said. "How come you aren't asleep?" Vander ran a successful security business and was married. The thought of Vander as a married businessman always made Sawyer shake his head. He still couldn't quite picture it.

Still, if someone had told him a few years back that he'd be a deputy sheriff on Maui, he probably would've laughed.

"My lovely wife is out on a case," Vander said. "She's due home soon."

So, Vander was waiting for his police detective wife. "Ah. Got it."

"How's Maui?"

"Good. The work is...interesting. Mainly tourists doing dumb stuff."

Vander gave a low chuckle. "Nice change of pace."

"Yeah."

Vander's team had lost three members on a mission. Sawyer had been one of the new recruits to replace them, coming out of the Navy Seals. Ghost Ops teams were made up of the best of the best of special forces from all branches of the military.

Vander and his men had been hurting after their loss, but they'd welcomed him. He wished he'd gotten to serve with them longer before Vander had retired. But Vander kept in touch, and Sawyer knew that the man kept his finger on the pulse of what all the old team members were doing.

Just recently, one of them, Ren Santoro, had his research ship attacked off the coast of Hawaii. The attackers had been after a top-secret military Navy research project.

Ren and a scientist had washed up on Molokai, on the run from Chinese operatives. Vander had called Sawyer, and asked him to help them. Sawyer had pulled in some favors and hauled ass to Molokai to help Ren.

His buddy had taken the attackers down, saved the military research, and fallen in love with the scientist.

"It's not too slow for you?" Vander asked. "There's always a place at Norcross Security, if you want it."

"Thanks, but I need to be here for now." Sawyer looked out at the ocean.

"I get it, Sawyer. I know what you went through. I also know you. I know you're battling a hefty dose of guilt, and survivor's guilt is the worst. None of it was your fault."

"My head knows that, but how I feel..."

"Yeah. That takes time to untangle." Vander paused. "It's better doing that when you're not alone."

Sawyer laughed. "I'm not alone. I've got Benny and Kalani, and her family. And there are a lot of them."

"I'm glad you've got family, but I'm talking about the female type of company."

"I don't need a woman."

"I thought that too, for a long time. Now she's my entire world. I'm fucking glad she pushed her way into my life."

Sawyer was happy for Vander, but it wasn't what he needed. Of course, that immediately made him think of red hair and blue eyes.

"You need anything, you just call," Vander said.

"Thanks, Vander. And if you ever want to take Brynn on a vacation, Maui is a great spot."

"I'll keep that in mind."

Once Vander had gone, Sawyer stayed there in the dark, staring at the ocean.

CHAPTER FOUR

Walking into the office, Sawyer enjoyed the blast of cool air from the air-conditioning.

The Sheriff Department office on Maui wasn't huge. The lower level was a large, open space filled with desks. The Maui Police Department had a bigger presence and a larger building in the center of Kahului. The two departments worked closely together.

A woman popped up from her desk. "Hey, how did it go?"

Leilani Sola was tiny, not even five feet tall and her Hawaiian heritage showed in her long, black hair and cute face. She looked fifteen, but he knew she was in her mid-twenties. She had a habit of wearing bright colors, and today was no exception. Her shirt was a lollipop pink that seared the eyes.

She was also the heart and soul of their little office. The woman could do just about anything.

"Fine. Got the prisoner delivered to the airport. He didn't cause any trouble."

"Because you were all scowly and intimidating."

"I don't scowl."

She snorted. "Yeah, right." She lifted a piece of paper off her desk. "There was a call for you. Tyler Janson was released from the hospital. He's going to be fine."

Sawyer smiled. "That's great news."

"His parents said to say thank you for the turtle toy you brought him yesterday. He loves it." She grinned at him. "You're just a big softie, aren't you, big guy?"

Sawyer grunted and headed for his desk. He dropped into his chair, and it creaked underneath him.

Leilani bustled over. "How come some woman hasn't snapped you up yet?"

"Not interested." Of course, his brain instantly provided him with an image of Hollis Stanton, naked. He blew out a breath. He was spending too much time thinking of creamy skin, blue eyes, and russet-red hair.

Leilani perched on the corner of his desk. "I have a friend from Oahu visiting—"

"No." This was a topic Leilani loved. She was forever trying to set him up.

She got a stubborn look on her face. "I want you happy, Sawyer. You deserve it."

"I am happy."

She rolled her dark eyes. "Fine. I want you getting some. You deserve that too. You know that regular sex leads to lower blood pressure, decreased stress, better sleep, better heart health—"

"Leilani..."

"You look tired," she said quietly. "I worry about you."

"I'm all right. I just didn't have a great night's sleep."

She wagged a finger at him. "Sex would help with that."

He groaned. She was like a damn terrier that wouldn't let go of a bone.

Deputy Sheriff Jesse Lee stopped beside them, file in hand. "Leilani playing matchmaker again?" The man was in his late fifties, with graying black hair and a barrel chest.

"I'm being a concerned friend," Leilani said.

"What have you got?" Sawyer looked at the file, hopeful Jesse had something that would get him out of the office again.

"PD called. Asked if we can take a look at a place out in Haiku. They think the people staying there might be linked to the drug case they're working. I'd go, but I'm due in court."

Sawyer stood and held out a hand. "I can take a look. Surveillance, only?"

"Yeah." Jesse slapped the file in Sawyer's hand. "They're building a case and hoping to take the entire ring down. They're peddling fentanyl on the island." Jesse's face hardened. "Been an uptick in fentanyl overdoses lately."

"I'll check it out." Haiku was on the other side of Paia. It wasn't too far away.

Leilani hopped off his desk. "I haven't forgotten our conversation."

"I have," Sawyer said.

She poked her tongue out at him, then headed for her desk.

Sawyer grabbed his keys and headed out. In the parking lot, there were several Sheriff Department SUVs parked in a row. He climbed into his, then opened the file. He scanned the details, then plugged the address into his navigation system.

Yes, his work now wasn't as dangerous or high-intensity as his Ghost Ops days, but it was still important. He liked knowing he was helping to keep the people of Maui, and the tourists who visited, safe.

He tossed the file on the passenger seat and started the engine. As he drove out onto the street, he wondered what Hollis was doing today.

No. No thinking about Hollis Stanton. His hands flexed on the wheel. He had work to do.

THIS. This was what she needed.

Hollis had done some research, and found a hiking trail just along the coast from Paia. She paused on the trail, gripped the straps of her small backpack, and breathed.

The air was warm and humid, and the lush scent of plants and flowers filled the air.

She continued on, her leg muscles pleasantly warm. She got to the top of the hill and smiled. There was a gorgeous view of the ocean and coastline. She exhaled. She could feel her blood pressure lowering.

It was easy to see why Sawyer had moved here and stayed. Of course, that made her thoughts turn to him, and not the view, or the interesting, complex script she'd read that morning.

It was clear he'd needed a haven after the military. She hadn't asked what branch he'd been in, and now she wondered how he looked in a uniform. If it was anything like the way he looked in his Sheriff Department uniform... She fanned herself. Here she was, drooling over a man like a teenage girl.

It had been a long time since she'd felt such an attraction to someone. It usually took her more time, until she really knew someone. Fame made it hard to trust people, which made it hard to get close to anyone.

Her nose wrinkled. She hadn't been the most trusting person before she'd become famous. She'd had a mom who was too busy and tired to be interested in her kids. Her father had flitted into her life once or twice, before he'd disappeared for good. She'd been close to her brother when they were young, but when he'd hit his teens, he'd gotten into drugs. Her heart squeezed.

And her last boyfriend had taught her that trusting someone was a risk that didn't always pay off.

Nope, she wasn't letting thoughts of Brody ruin her morning.

She paused to take a drink of water, then munched on a granola bar. She pulled out her camera and snapped some pictures of the view. It was stunning. She hadn't passed a single person on the trail. It felt like she had the entire island to herself.

She reached the end of the hike loop and sat on a rock, watching the waves below.

This Reuben situation was stressful, but she realized

THE HERO SHE DESERVES

that on top of it, she was already close to burnout with her work.

She had an Oscar sitting on her shelf at home. She got paid an eye-watering amount of money to star in films. She got to pick the roles she wanted. The days of taking anything that came her way to build her resume were long gone.

She knew she could slow down. She just wasn't sure how to go about it.

She tapped a finger on her leg. Slowing down didn't sit well with her Type-A personality. Since she was a kid, she'd been driven to get good grades, star in the best part in the play, win at all her sports. To claw her way out of an unstable, poor childhood.

To prove what, Hollis? And to whom?

She was financially stable now, but maybe she felt like if she turned down roles, they might dry up altogether. And everyone would realize she was an imposter. That she was still the poor kid with her brother's hand-me-down shoes, tangled red hair, and no one to help her with her homework.

Only one person had helped her with her homework. Dave. He'd married her Mom when Hollis had been thirteen. He'd been a firefighter and worked odd shifts. That meant he often looked after her when her Mom was at work. He'd helped her with her dreaded math homework, and he'd gotten her into watching old movies. She smiled. Some of her favorite memories were curled up on the couch watching *Casablanca* or *The Wizard of Oz* with Dave.

She knew that Dave would be proud of everything

she'd achieved. And pissed she was running on fumes while some asshole was scaring her.

Okay, enough overthinking. She rose and set off back down the trail. What she really needed was sex—hard, hot, forget-your-name sex. She laughed. It was funny, since she was pretty sure she'd never actually had sex like that.

Sawyer popped into her head because, of course, he did. The vision of his bare chest and all those lickable muscles was hard to shake.

A twig snapped somewhere behind her. Startled out of her sexy daydream, she whirled, expecting to see some hikers.

There was nobody there.

Frowning, she scanned the trees.

With a shake of her head, she kept walking. It must have been an animal. Her thoughts turned to her plans. She'd stop in Paia for lunch, and maybe visit Island Brew again.

There was loud rustling in the nearby bushes.

She froze. "Hello?"

Nothing. The wind played with a few wisps of her hair that had escaped her ponytail. Tension crept in, coiling in her belly.

"Who's there?"

More rustling, but no answer. Maybe it was an animal?

Or someone was following her.

Hollis set off at a half jog. She wanted to get back to her car.

In the distance behind her, she was sure she heard a

voice. She picked up speed, her heart beating hard. Then she heard footsteps pounding.

Someone was following her.

She broke into a run. *Oh, God.* She glanced back, and spotted a hint of a black shirt in the greenery.

She ran faster. She'd always liked distance running at school. She stumbled over some overgrown tree roots, flailed, but managed to catch her balance. She fumbled to get her phone out of her pocket, breathing heavily.

She swiped the screen, then pressed it to her ear.

He answered on the first ring. "Hollis?"

"Sawyer, oh God..." She gripped the phone tightly.

"What's wrong? Did you set your toaster on fire?"

"Sawyer..." A sob escaped her.

"What is it?" His tone sharpened.

"I'm on a hiking trail. Someone's chasing me."

He cursed. "What trail?"

She tried to think. Some of the Hawaiian names sounded so similar. "I'm just north of Paia. Um at...the Ho'okipa Beach trail. Near the lookout."

"I'm not far from you. I'm coming."

"Hurry. *Please.*"

"Get to your car."

"I'm trying." She glanced back, and could hear a body moving through the vegetation. "I can hear them."

"Get to the trailhead, Hollis. You can do it."

"All right." She tucked the phone back in her pocket, and lifted her chin. *Get to her car.* She sure as hell wasn't going to let some asshole terrorize her.

SAWYER STEPPED ON THE GAS, his department SUV roaring down the road toward Ho'okipa Beach.

He gripped the wheel. He had to get to Hollis.

Maybe an overzealous fan had recognized her? Maybe whatever she was hiding from had caught up with her?

The thought of her, alone, in danger, had his heart pounding. He pushed the SUV for more speed.

Finally, he saw the sign for the trail and lookout, and wrenched the wheel. The tires crunched over gravel, and he pulled to a stop.

As he got out, he noted there were no other cars in the lot except for Hollis's rental.

Where was she?

He strode forward, scanning around. Then he heard a sound, and Hollis sprinted out of the trees.

Panic was written all over her face. When she saw him, relief was like the sun breaking over the horizon.

"*Sawyer,*" she panted.

Then she was in his arms.

He caught her, his arms wrapping around her. "I've got you."

"Sawyer..." She was out of breath.

"Take it easy." He ran his hand up her back. "Just breathe."

He lifted his head to take in the trees again. He didn't see anyone after her, but he stayed alert.

Hollis was shaking.

"Come on." He urged her over to a wooden fence. He sat and pulled her down beside him.

She leaned into him, like she needed the contact. He put an arm around her.

"You're safe now."

She looked back at the path. "You must have scared them off."

He tipped her face up. It was still pale. "How are you doing?"

She smiled, but it was still a little shaky. "Oh, you know, girl goes for a peaceful hike, and ends up getting a little extra cardio."

He cupped her jaw. "You'll be fine."

She nodded. "I will. I always am."

"I'm going to take a look around."

Her hands gripped his arm. "You'll be careful?"

His lips quirked. He'd been a Navy SEAL, then in Ghost Ops, and now a deputy sheriff. No one ever reminded him to be careful.

"I've got it. Now, I want you to sit in my SUV, with the doors locked."

She swallowed. "Okay."

He got her settled in the passenger seat and locked the doors.

Then Sawyer turned and strode up the trail. As he followed it up the gentle slope, he didn't see anyone. He scanned around. Nothing. He went on a little farther, until he reached a muddy patch of ground. Hollis's neat shoe print was obvious.

There were no other prints.

He checked off the trail, looking for any sign of whoever had scared her.

Nothing. No sign of anyone but Hollis on the path.

With a frown, he headed back to the SUV. He didn't want to leave her alone too long. He felt a faint prickle on the back of his neck, and turned fast.

There was no one there.

Some birds squawked loudly in the trees.

He headed back to the parking area. Another car had just pulled in, and he saw some young hikers getting out. They nodded as he walked past them.

Before he reached the SUV, Hollis opened the door. "Did you find him?"

Sawyer shook his head. "I found your footprints, but no others. There was no sign of anyone else."

Her shoulders sagged, and she looked away. "You think I imagined it." Her voice was dull.

He grabbed her hand. "I didn't say that."

She didn't respond.

"Someone tell you that you're imagining things?" he asked.

She let out a long breath. "It doesn't matter. I'm a high-strung actress, we love making things up and being the center of attention."

And being sarcastic. "Hollis—"

"It's okay, Sawyer. Thanks for coming. I'm sorry to waste your time." She hopped out of the SUV, and turned toward her car.

"Hey." He grabbed her hand again and pulled her to face him. "If *anything* worries you, big or small, you call me. I have no idea what happened on that trail, but just because there's no evidence, doesn't mean that someone wasn't there."

Her lips parted. Her perfect, kissable lips.

"Thanks, Sawyer," she whispered.

"We're having a barbecue on the beach this evening. My cousin and some of his family. You should come."

"A barbecue? Like a luau?"

"Sort of. It's just family. Luaus are usually to celebrate special events, with traditional dress and entertainment. This is just family sharing good food and drink, and a bonfire."

"I'd love to come."

Sawyer really liked seeing the happy look on her face.

"Good." *Not good.* It was a dumb idea to spend more time with her. "From Archer's place, just head out to the beach, then turn right. You'll see the bonfire. Benny always makes a big one."

"It sounds great. Thanks, Sawyer."

CHAPTER FIVE

Hollis sat on the couch reading a new script. She liked the story. The character was strong, yet flawed, and didn't trust easily.

It was a Western saga, which was new for her. She liked Elsa—a tough, confident woman making her own way in a challenging world, who also falls for a stoic lawman.

Hmm. It seemed she and Elsa had a thing for stoic men of the law.

There were also some Native American characters who were going to be played by some great up-and-coming Native American actors. The lawman was being played by an actor she respected. The female director attached was brilliant. Hollis had worked with her before.

She lowered the script and smiled. She felt good. The morning's drama was long over, thank God. With some perspective, she was sure she'd just panicked over some noises and imagined things. She felt a buzz of excitement for this script, and for the up-and-coming barbecue on the beach.

She glanced at her watch. She needed to get ready.

Setting the script aside, she headed for the bedroom. She loved Archer's house. She couldn't believe he didn't come here more often. In the walk-in closet, she studied the clothes she'd brought with her. Sawyer and his cousin's family were going to be attending tonight. He'd told her it would be small and casual. She chewed on her lip and pulled some clothes out.

That was too casual. She tossed the trousers on the bed. That was too dressy. She hung the dress back up.

She wanted to look good, but not like she was trying too hard.

There. She pulled a pretty, red, wrap dress out. Casual but nice.

She slipped on a black bikini, then pulled on the dress and tied the belt.

Perfect. She didn't wear red a lot, but she didn't *not* wear it. She pulled her hair up in a messy bun, and kept her makeup natural. She was well aware that someone could recognize her tonight, but she couldn't wear sunglasses and a cap at nighttime. Hopefully, Sawyer's friends wouldn't feel the need to post her picture on social media.

Since the barbeque was on the beach, she wouldn't wear too much jewelry. Maybe just her favorite silver bracelet. It had been a gift from Dave when she'd landed her first movie role. Sure, it had only been a tiny part in a teen flick, but it had meant the world to her. Dave had acted like she'd already won an Oscar. Unsurprisingly, her mom hadn't given her anything.

She pulled a face and headed over to the dresser. She opened her jewelry case and skimmed her gaze over the few pieces she'd been wearing lately.

But no bracelet.

She frowned. "Crap." She remembered putting it right there last night. She searched the bedroom, then the bathroom.

No bracelet.

Feeling a little panicked, she searched the kitchen and living room.

"*Dammit.*" She'd be upset if she'd lost it.

She hadn't worn it today. She distinctly remembered setting it on the dresser last night. She felt a tinge of unease, but shook it off. No one had broken in. Why would someone take a bracelet? There was more expensive jewelry on offer.

She glanced at her watch. Crap, she needed to go, or she'd be late. She'd look for the bracelet later, and hope she'd just dropped it somewhere in the house.

She slipped on some cute, strappy sandals and headed out.

The sunset was gorgeous. She hit the beach and turned right, but her gaze stayed on the way the golden light changed the colors of the water. The sound of voices ahead caught her ear.

She spotted the glimmer of a bonfire, and smiled. She was excited to see Sawyer.

She shouldn't be. She wasn't here to find a man.

Brody, the last man she'd dated, had left her more than a little wary.

As she got closer to the cookout, she noted the big crowd. She tensed. This didn't look small. There was a bonfire, and food roasting on it. And lots of people sitting on chairs and blankets.

Sawyer had said it was just his cousin and family, but this looked far bigger than that. She slowed her steps. What if people recognized her and caused a fuss?

Then she saw Sawyer's large form emerge from the throng, walking toward her.

"Hi," he said.

He was wearing khaki cargo shorts, and a black shirt that clung to his body. The band on the sleeves was tight on his biceps.

Hollis tipped her head back. "Hi." Her gaze flicked to the crowd. "Um...I didn't realize there would be so many people."

He took her hand. "Benny's wife has a *big* family. When they grill on the beach, everyone comes. Aunts, uncles, cousins, second cousins."

"Sawyer..."

"I promise no one will bother you." He pulled her close. "I won't let them."

Her heart skipped a beat. When was the last time someone had shielded her, cared for her? Or at least someone who wasn't on her payroll. "There's always someone willing to sell a photo of me."

"I already talked with everyone. That's not going to happen."

He seemed so sure, but she'd been burned too many

times before. She walked with him, and he led her over to a blanket.

"Benny," Sawyer said.

A man turned toward them. He had on a gray T-shirt that said *Born to Windsurf, Forced to Work*.

"This is Hollis," Sawyer said.

Benny smiled. The man looked nothing like Sawyer. He was shorter, with a lean body, and beach-blond hair that brushed his shoulders. "Welcome, Hollis. Grab some food before it's gone. This crowd is never shy, and they are *always* willing to eat."

"Thanks."

"Sit," Sawyer told her. "I'll get you a plate of food." He hesitated. "Ah, you don't just eat salad, do you?"

She laughed. "No, I like meat, and I'm always willing to eat. It just means I work out more."

He nodded.

She sat on the blanket and watched him move to the food table. She couldn't take her eyes off that big, powerful body. People stopped to talk with him, and a few older women patted his beard-covered cheek. One even patted his ass.

Hollis giggled.

He returned with two plates, and a glass of white wine. He handed one plate and the glass to her.

"Thanks. I should've brought a plate of something."

"We're more than covered for food." He sat down beside her. "Now, eat."

The food looked delicious, the ocean was beautiful, and the man beside her mouthwatering.

"Thanks for inviting me," she murmured.

He smiled. "Thanks for coming."

HE KNEW the food was good, but he barely tasted anything.

Sawyer watched the stars appear in the sky, and firelight flicker over Hollis's face.

She was finally relaxed, and had surprised him by eating nearly everything on the plate. She clearly enjoyed it.

"It's so beautiful here," she said.

He kept his gaze on her. "Yeah, it is."

She smiled at him. "I can understand why you came here. And stayed." She paused, pushing one toe through the sand. "It must have been a huge change of pace."

"That's an understatement."

Two young boys raced past, kicking up sand.

Sawyer shot out an arm and caught one of them. "Hey, you need to watch where you're running." He tipped the boy upside down.

The kid giggled. "Sorry, Uncle Sawyer."

Sawyer set Kalani's nephew on his feet and tickled him. "Careful, or I'll arrest you."

That got Sawyer a wide, unconcerned grin. The boy raced off to find his partner in crime.

When he looked over, Hollis was smiling at him. She leaned back, her hands in the sand. "Do you miss the military?"

"Parts of it." He was quiet a moment. "It was challenging, and I liked that. I liked pushing myself, and I was good at it. And I believed in what I was doing. In protecting my country."

"What branch?"

"Navy. I was a SEAL."

Her eyes widened. "Wow. That's tough work."

"I enjoyed it. And being on a team, with people I could trust. That's special. But eventually, all the things I'd seen, the fights I'd been in... I knew I had to get out."

She nodded, her face serious.

"I wasn't sure what I wanted to do. I don't have family in Montana anymore, and I didn't want to go to Florida where my mom is. Benny invited me to Maui."

She glanced over at Benny. He had an arm around his beautiful, dark-haired wife.

"They saved me," Sawyer said quietly. "Benny, Kalani, her family. When I first arrived, I was always getting dragged out to dinner, or a family birthday party, or windsurfing. Still am. They didn't let me sit and brood. Much."

Her lips tipped. "I bet you're good at brooding."

He laughed, and sipped his beer. "I have my moments."

On the other side of the fire, music started. Uncle Duke was strumming his battered guitar, and a young man—one of Kalani's cousins—started playing a ukelele. A moment later, an auntie started singing in Hawaiian.

"They're good." Hollis swayed in time to the music.

He knew she'd worked with some of the best composers and singers for her movies. "You love Hollywood?"

"No, I hate Hollywood."

His eyebrows shot up.

She pulled a face. "It's all so fake and cutthroat. But I love acting. Sometimes I think it saved my sanity. I had a stepfather for a while. A really great guy. He was a fire-fighter, who didn't mind inheriting an awkward, teenage stepdaughter. He loved classic movies and got me watching them. Movie night with Dave was one of my favorite things. We'd make popcorn and fight over the remote."

Sawyer smiled. "What was his favorite movie?"

"Butch Cassidy and the Sundance Kid."

"And yours?"

"I couldn't just pick one, but I am partial to *The Wizard of Oz*. I'd kill for a pair of shiny, red shoes. Plus, Dorothy's hair looked red to me. Another sign."

"You don't see Dave anymore."

Her face fell. Sawyer couldn't stop himself from reaching out and covering her hand with his.

"I had Dave for almost five years. He was the first and only person to tell me that he believed in me." She shot Sawyer a sad smile. "Then, my brother died of a drug overdose, and one month after that, Dave had a heart attack. I lost them both."

"Shit, I'm so sorry, Hollis."

"Thanks." She pinned on a smile. "I learned a long time ago that life isn't always fair. That sometimes, things suck."

"Yeah." He'd had his share of that. "SEALs have a saying, embrace the suck. That the only easy day was yesterday."

She laughed. "Not quite something you want

stitched on a pillow, but I sometimes feel like the only easy day was months ago."

He stroked her fingers with his. "You going to tell me what you're running from?"

Instantly, she tensed up. *Shit.* He was sorry he'd pushed.

"Nothing." She shrugged a shoulder. "Like I said, I was burned out and running on fumes. Maui seemed like a good place to recharge."

She was a good actress, but even she couldn't hide the entire truth. Eventually, he'd get it out of her. When she trusted him.

"And there's always paparazzi and overzealous fans," she added. "Hazard of the job."

"None of those here."

She tilted her head. "Oh, you're not a fan?"

"I like your movies. I'm a fan, just not overzealous."

He detected a faint flush on her cheeks. He found it attractive as hell that she could still blush. That she wasn't too jaded by Hollywood.

"So no boyfriend, huh?" he asked.

She shook her head and sipped her wine. "The last guy I dated was a Hollywood agent. I thought he was charming, handsome, driven."

Hell, Sawyer was none of those things. His hands tightened on his beer bottle.

"Right up to the point where he sold a tell-all exposé about me to a tabloid."

Sawyer winced. "Asshole."

"Of epic proportions. He also included a photo that

he'd snapped of me, topless, in my own private swimming pool."

Sawyer's hand clenched in a fist. "Did you sue his ass?"

"I did. I don't sue often. It's just not worth it. If I sued whenever someone spread a lie about me, it would be like playing a whack-a-mole game. But this was personal, and I felt so violated." She pushed her hair back over her shoulder. "Luckily, I have great breasts, so at least they looked good splashed on the cover of a gazillion magazines." Her tone was as dry as dust.

He couldn't help himself. His gaze dropped, noting the cleavage revealed by her red dress. "A silver lining."

But he guessed that the motherfucker had rattled her trust.

He spotted a couple of Kalani's young cousins hovering nearby, gazes flitting to Hollis. They cautiously approached, phones in hand.

"No photos," he warned. "Hollis is on vacation."

The girls both nodded.

"Sure thing, Sawyer," the older of the pair said. "Um, Ms. Stanton, I'm such a fan."

The other girl nodded and swallowed, clearly speechless.

"Can we...get your autograph?" the first girl asked hopefully.

Hollis smiled. "Sure thing. You have a pen."

The girls pulled out a pen and paper. As she signed, Hollis chatted easily with them, asking them what movies they enjoyed.

"Thank you so much!" Beaming, the girls hurried off.

"Thanks for doing that," Sawyer said.

She nodded. "I like interacting with fans."

The music changed to something more upbeat. A few couples started dancing on the sand.

"Come on, you two." Benny appeared and hauled Hollis to her feet.

Sawyer took her arm and led her toward the dancers. Benny went to claim his wife.

Clearing his throat, Sawyer pulled her closer. "I'm not much of a dancer."

"Yet you're doing it." She leaned into him.

"Any excuse to hold you close."

She nibbled on her lip, which gave him ideas, and her gaze drifted over his face. Then she rested her cheek against his chest, and they swayed to the music. The moon rose up over the ocean.

"God, it's gorgeous." She sighed. "You can't see the stars in LA, and the moon doesn't look anything like this. So clear and bright."

He wanted to hold her closer, but he didn't. There were dozens of reasons jumbling in his head why he needed to keep some distance from her.

She was an actress, she wasn't from here, and she was way out of his league. And he had his own suitcase of baggage.

But they kept dancing, swaying to their own song.

People slowly started to leave the party. Parents ushered tired kids off the sand, couples drifted off, arm in arm, and the older family members hugged and kissed.

"I should probably get home," she murmured.

Sawyer took her hand. "I'll walk you back."

CHAPTER SIX

S he was so aware of Sawyer as he walked beside her.
The beach was shrouded in darkness, with just
the moonlight glinting on the water.

It was romantic.

Everything Hollis had learned about Sawyer Lane,
she liked. She rarely got a chance to get to really know
people, without fame getting in the way. People always
wanted the glamorous actress, not her. Regular, old
Hollis.

Sawyer didn't seem wowed by her fame at all.

She liked that. A lot.

"Your family is so fun," she said.

"They're not mine, they're Benny's, but they sort of
adopted me."

"That makes them even more special."

"Yeah. But they can be nosy as hell sometimes.
Beware a matchmaking auntie on the war path."

Hollis grinned. "Have they tried to fix you up with
some nice, young girls?"

ANNA HACKETT

"Yeah. A few times."

"But it didn't stick?" She found her chest hitching as she waited for his answer.

"Wasn't interested." He glanced her way, his face in shadow. "After I got out, I...well, I was a little worried that part of me had gone to sleep."

Her heart hit her ribs. "And now?"

"It's awake now."

Her belly tightened. Did he mean her? She licked her lips. Neither of them wanted a relationship. Neither of them were looking for it.

Hell, her life was a giant mess right now. The last thing she needed was a man. But she couldn't deny the attraction between them.

Her house came into view, and they walked up the steps and past the pool.

"I appreciate you walking me back."

"I didn't want you accidentally starting a fire."

"Ha-ha." She unlocked the sliding door, nerves alive in her belly. When was the last time she'd had nerves over a man?

Then again, she'd never met a man like Sawyer.

She already trusted him, and he was so...big, solid.

"Would you like to come in for a drink?" She turned and their gazes met.

"Yes."

"Great. Great." *Act normal, Hols.* She stepped inside and dropped her handbag on the floor.

He followed her, and instantly it felt like he took up the entire room. He closed the sliding door and locked it.

"What have you got to drink?" he asked.

She stared at his lips. She wasn't entirely sure what was in the fridge. She couldn't think. She felt hot, and her clothes felt too tight. "I have no idea."

He took a step closer.

Her pulse went crazy. "Um, what do you want?"

He took another step toward her and now she felt the heat radiating off him.

"You really want me to answer that?" His voice was low, gritty. "Because it's not a drink."

Her heart hit her ribs, and desire flooded her belly. Hollis decided to stop thinking and just feel.

She lunged for him, but he was already moving.

He grabbed her and hauled her against his chest. Her lips touched his, and she moaned, and slid her hands into his hair. She did her best to climb his muscular body.

Sawyer's hands slid under her ass, and she wrapped her legs around his waist. He was so strong. She was tall, but he held her securely. She deepened the kiss, and this time he groaned. Their tongues tangled and she squirmed against him. Her sensitive spots rubbed against hard muscle.

She pulled her mouth from his, panting. "*Now*. I can't wait any longer."

He took a step, his gaze scanning the room. Then he marched across to the dining room table and set her on it.

Need—hot and frantic—pumped inside her. She needed to feel her skin against his. She needed to be close to this man. She reached for his shirt, unfastening the buttons. She made a sound of frustration. It was taking too long. She gripped the shirt and yanked. Buttons went flying, pinging on the tile floor.

"Faster, Sawyer." She leaned forward to kiss his glorious, bare chest.

"Shit. Hollis—" He pulled her face up, and his mouth was on hers. The kiss was hard, savage.

Excitement flooded her. He wanted her the same way she wanted him.

He untied her dress and pushed it open, baring her bikini. He growled. An honest to God growl that lit her up.

He yanked her top down, letting her breasts spill over the top.

"These gorgeous breasts." He cupped them. "I could spend all night right here."

"Later," she panted. "I need you inside me."

He swore under his breath, then his hands went to the fly of his shorts. "Whatever you want, Hollis, I'll give it to you."

As he flicked his shorts open, she attacked his chest again with nips and kisses. She smoothed her hands over his hard abs. He was pure fantasy, but oh so real. Warm skin and hard muscle.

When he shoved his shorts and boxers down, a rock-hard, sizable cock sprang free.

Oh. Her pulse tripped.

As she watched, he wrapped a hand around it and stroked. She felt a flood of damp between her thighs and reached out, her hand joining his.

He hissed out a breath. "Hollis, gorgeous, careful. I think I've wanted you from the moment I first saw you, beautifully naked. I've been half hard for days."

She liked hearing that. Her belly coiled.

"If you keep your hand on me, then what's coming will be hard and rough." His voice was all grit. "You'll feel me for days."

More need washed through her. She squirmed on the cool surface of the table. "I want hard. I *need* rough."

"You need me to take away the ache?"

She nodded.

His hand moved to her bikini bottoms. He pulled them firm against her, the fabric digging into her slick, swollen flesh.

"*God.*" She moaned, her head falling back, and she parted her legs. She knew he'd see how wet her bikini bottoms were.

With a hard yank, he pulled the ties at the side free, and pulled the bikini bottoms away. His big hand gripped her hips, and yanked her to the edge of the table.

She gripped the table for leverage, and she watched as he fisted his cock and pressed it between her legs.

They both groaned.

Then he froze. "Shit, I don't have a condom."

He hadn't carried one with him tonight. Hadn't expected to score with the famous actress. She felt something shift inside her, another burst of trust. Sawyer Lane was a good guy.

She met his gaze. "I'm safe. Really safe. I get regular checkups, I have an IUD, and... It's been a while. I'm guessing it's the same for you?"

A muscle in his jaw flexed. "I haven't been with a woman since I got out of the military. Had several medicals since then."

Her lips parted. "You haven't been with anyone?"

"I didn't want to be with anyone until you." His voice was low.

"I need you, Sawyer." She needed him badly.

He surged forward with a low, masculine sound.

That hard thrust filled her. She cried out, arching into him. The table scraped on the floor.

She was full of Sawyer.

DAMN, she felt good. Desire pumped thick and hot in his veins. Hollis was sweet and tight, her inner muscles clamping down on him. Her nails bit into his shoulders.

"Don't... Move." She dragged in a breath. "You're a lot to take."

"Hang on to me, gorgeous."

She gripped his arms. He slid one hand between their bodies and found the swollen nub of her clit. He stroked in steady circles.

"*Oh.*" She let out a low, sexy sound. Her head dropped back, showcasing that long, graceful neck. She let out a whimper.

Sawyer had to move.

He started thrusting. She panted his name, holding on tight. The table scraped on the floor again, but he didn't care.

The only thing that existed for him was Hollis. The way she felt, the sounds she made.

He thrust faster, and felt his impending orgasm getting closer. He strummed her clit, his senses awash with the feel of her and the scent of her arousal.

"Let me hear how much you want my cock, Hollis. Let me watch you come on it."

She let out a long, low moan, then her body clenched tight. She cried out his name, her heels digging into his back.

He'd never seen anything as beautiful as Hollis coming.

He wasn't going to last much longer.

"Look at me," he growled.

Dazed blue eyes met his.

He kept his gaze locked on hers as his own climax hit. He groaned. *Fuck.* He poured his release inside her.

Then there was only their harsh panting and the slickness of their skin gluing them together.

"That was a hell of a nightcap," he murmured.

She laughed.

God, he loved that sound. He speared his hands into her hair, then he pressed a slow kiss to her lips.

She blinked and looked almost confused.

"You with me?" he asked.

She nodded, her hair tumbled, her face flushed. "My thigh muscles are burning a little. You're better than the gym workout."

Now Sawyer laughed. He eased out of her, watching as she bit her lip.

Her fingers tightened on his arms. "If you let me go, I'll slide off the table and land in a melted puddle on the floor."

"I'm not letting you go." He hitched his shorts up and then lifted her into his arms.

"Hmm." She slid an arm along his shoulders. "This is nice."

"I know you've been carried before. I've seen it in the movies." He headed down the hall toward the bedroom.

She made a scoffing sound. "Yes, and it's always highly choreographed, and no one's ever carried me this far."

He stepped into the shadowed bedroom.

"Um, I need to clean up," she said.

He set her down. "I'll do it."

Her eyes widened. He cupped her jaw, and then one breast. Her nipple pebbled.

"I'm not done with you yet, gorgeous."

"All right," she whispered.

"I can do better than a quick fuck on the table. I want to show you that."

She cleared her throat. "I was pretty impressed with that."

He rubbed his lips over hers. "You haven't seen anything yet."

She shivered. "Sawyer, I want you to stay."

He took her hand and squeezed. "No place I'd rather be."

CHAPTER SEVEN

There was nothing sexier than watching Sawyer kneeling beside the bed with his head between her legs.

Hollis panted, undulating her hips against his oh-so-clever mouth. He had one of her thighs in a tight grip, and the other she wrapped around his head.

"Sawyer, oh God—"

He worked a finger inside her. She was a little tender from their night together. She'd discovered the former Navy SEAL had stamina. A lot of it.

His finger filled her, his tongue lapping at her clit. And she couldn't think anymore. She was racing headfirst toward a magnificent orgasm.

"*Sawyer.*" His name was filled with pleading.

She came hard, her cries filling the room and her body shaking. She collapsed back on the bed.

When her blurred vision cleared, she looked down at a smiling and very smug looking Sawyer.

"Good morning." His voice was a deep rumble.

"It sure is," she replied.

He ran a hand up her thigh and squeezed. "Unfortunately, I need to get home to change and then head to work."

"Okay." Part of her didn't want him to leave. It looked like her good morning was over. "We didn't get much sleep last night." And she'd be busy reliving the memories of what they'd done instead of sleeping all day long.

He shrugged one broad shoulder. "I don't sleep much. I'm used to running on catnaps."

She frowned, but he was already pulling away to grab his clothes.

As he got dressed, she pulled herself out of bed. Her legs were deliciously wobbly. She pulled on her favorite, silky, white robe covered in large hibiscus flowers. She tied her hair up in a messy knot and turned. "I'd offer to make you some coffee, but my coffee machine self-imploded."

He smiled, and her belly tightened. A smile shouldn't affect her so much.

"I'll grab one from Island Brew later. The stuff we call coffee in the office is bad." His gaze ran over her face. "God, you're beautiful."

Warmth filled her. She'd heard that phrase so many times before, usually when she was dolled up for an event, after hours of hair and makeup.

Not when she was makeup-free, with tangled hair, and stubble burn on her neck and jaw.

"Thank you," she murmured.

He pulled her in close, his arms wrapping around her. "You have plans today?"

"A little shopping in Paia."

"There are some great stores. One-of-a-kind boutiques selling clothes and art."

"Maybe I'll find a new coffee machine. I owe Archer one. And once I get home, I've got some scripts to read, then I'm going to go down to the beach for a swim."

His finger traced over her cheekbone. "I'll drop by later."

"I'd like that."

He tugged her up onto her toes and his lips touched hers. She opened her mouth, and he deepened the kiss. Seconds turned to minutes. His hand clenched on her ass, and she pressed into him.

With a groan, he stepped back, reluctance stamped all over his face. "You are pure temptation."

He held her hand as they walked to the door. She stood in the doorway, and watched him head for the path she guessed led to his place. He gave her a wave and disappeared into the trees.

She shouldn't feel like the sun had disappeared behind a cloud. Hollis straightened her shoulders and headed back to the kitchen. She set about making a yogurt parfait for breakfast.

Her cellphone rang and when she saw Tave's name, she tapped the speaker. "Morning."

"Morning." Her agent paused. "You sound chipper."

"It's a beautiful morning, the sun is shining, and I'm making a delicious yogurt parfait." She tossed some berries onto her creation.

Tave was quiet for a moment. "You got laid."

"What?" *How the hell could he know?*

"I assume Detective Hottie charmed his way into your bed."

"It's *Deputy* Hottie, and his name is Sawyer."

"I knew it."

Hollis stuck her spoon in the yogurt and leaned against the island. "And he didn't charm me. Not the way you mean. He's a...really good guy. Looks out for me, pays attention, walked me home. I'd given up believing men like him existed."

"And he has a hard bod and an energetic cock?"

She choked on a laugh. "Tave!"

"That's a yes. Well, as both your agent and friend, I'm glad you're getting some good sex."

"It wasn't good, it was stupendous." Heat filled her cheeks at the memories. "We didn't get much sleep. I didn't know people had sex like this."

"Now you're just gloating."

"Maybe. A little."

"You've earned it after Bastard Brody."

Not even the thought of her ex could dim her mood. "How's LA?"

"Fine. Hot and the traffic sucks. Did you read any of the scripts I sent with you?"

"I did. I really like the Lehman one."

"Me too. I'll put out some feelers on the Elsa role. I'm going to courier over some other ones I think you'll like."

"Thanks, Tave." She ate a spoonful of yogurt.

"I've also been keeping tabs on Reuben."

The yogurt curdled in her stomach. "I want you to be careful. He's dangerous."

"I'm not making it obvious. He's still in LA, going

about his business. He's drumming up support for a new movie."

While she was hiding out in Hawaii, half terrified.

"The new security system's been installed at your place," Tave continued. "I got them to do a full sweep. They didn't find any cameras or bugs."

"Thanks," she whispered.

"It's going to be okay, Hols. You aren't alone."

She'd always been alone. Her mom had been too busy and worn out to be there for her. Her father didn't even bother to stick around. Her brother had lost himself in drugs. Dave had died. The one guarantee in life was that you best get used to standing on your own two feet.

"I'm sure I blew all of this out of proportion," she said. "This will all blow over."

God, she hoped she wasn't lying to herself.

"All right, Red. Go enjoy the ocean, but don't get that million-dollar skin sunburned. You have a photoshoot for Dior coming up and they don't want peeling skin."

"I'll put sunscreen on, Dad."

"And have some more hot sex with your deputy. It's good stress relief."

She laughed.

"Talk soon, Hols."

"Bye, Tave."

After she finished her breakfast, she headed for the bathroom. She needed to shower, change, and then she was going shopping.

After a quick shower, she stood in the closet. Her disguise for today was a cute straw hat, capri pants, and a blue T-shirt. She kept her hair tucked away under the hat and then went looking for her favorite bracelet again. Still no sign of it. She hoped it turned up soon.

Oh, she needed some perfume. She backtracked to the bathroom, and caught her reflection in the mirror. She looked happy, relaxed. She smiled. Clearly all she needed was Sawyer inside her, touching her.

A delicate flush of color filled her cheeks. She looked forward to seeing him later. Maybe she'd cook dinner for him. She wasn't much of a chef, but she had a few things in her repertoire. Sawyer struck her as a steak kind of guy. Hmm, maybe she'd make her pepper steak stir fry with some fresh greens and rice.

She reached for her perfume, but it wasn't there. She frowned. It had been on the vanity sink in the bathroom last night. She'd worn a spritz of it to the barbecue.

She searched around the bathroom but there was no sign of the bottle.

Now she felt a strong skitter of unease. Her bracelet was missing, and now her perfume.

There was no one but you and Sawyer in the house. No one knows you're here.

Hollis rubbed her temple. Someone had followed her on the hiking trail. Now her things were missing. Okay, why would someone take her things? That made no sense.

Except if they wanted to freak you out.

With a shake of her head, she stalked out of the bathroom. Maybe it was a kid from the barbecue on the beach? Wanting a Hollis Stanton souvenir. Or maybe she'd just misplaced them.

She wasn't going to cower and be afraid. She'd look

around for the bracelet and perfume later. She snatched up her keys and handbag.

For now, she was going to head into Paia, get a coffee from Island Brew, then go shopping. Later, she'd cook dinner for a delicious hunk of a man, and maybe have more earth-shattering sex.

Instantly, she felt better. She got in her car and headed for town.

SIPPING HER CHILI-CINNAMON LATTE—YES, it sounded weird but it was fabulous—Hollis walked down the main street of Paia. Kiana really was a coffee maestro.

She loved the laid-back vacation vibe of the town. The wooden storefronts were charming and filled with gorgeous things. As she'd been making Hollis's unique latte, Kiana had proudly shared some of the town's history, from its sugar plantation heyday to today. Her family had lived in Paia for a long time.

Hollis paused to look in a store window, filled with cute glass bottles, perfumes, lotions, and bowls filled with colorful rocks and semi-precious stones.

She needed a new perfume. She scowled. Hers had to be in the house somewhere. She pushed open the shop door and a bell tinkled. As she moved inside, the smell of incense hit her.

An older man with distinguished gray threaded through his dark hair, and the most hideous Hawaiian shirt she'd ever seen, brushed past her on his way out.

"Hello." An older woman in a long, flowing skirt, and

with long, curly ash-blonde hair appeared from a back room. She gave off a strong hippie vibe. "Welcome to Kaleidoscope." The woman eyed her. "You have a very strong aura."

"Oh, um...thanks?"

The woman smiled. "It's a good thing. I can sense that you're energetic, passionate, creative." She cocked her head. "You are showing some worry and stress. You're afraid of something."

Goosebumps peppered Hollis's arms. "Aren't we all?"

"Luckily, I also detect love on the horizon. You have new shades of pink. I believe it's with someone you can trust."

Now Hollis got goosebumps *on* her goosebumps. "I'm not looking for love today, just some perfume. Maybe something Hawaiian?"

The woman beamed. "We have some wonderful blends. With essential oils made right here on the island. Come. I'm Lavender, by the way."

"Holli."

Fifteen minutes later, Hollis stepped out of Kaleidoscope with a frangipani-based perfume, and Lavender's proclamation to trust the man who was adding color to her aura.

With a shake of her head, she headed down the street. She paused to look in other shop windows, admiring the clothing and artwork.

A prickle started on the back of her neck.

She turned her head, scanning both sides of the street. No one appeared to be looking at her.

She continued onto the next shop, but the sensation of being watched didn't abate. She hunched her shoulders, walking faster. She'd planned to find somewhere that sold coffee machines, but that could wait. Maybe it was time to get back to her car and head home.

She nearly collided with someone on the sidewalk.

"Sorry!" She looked up at Sawyer's cousin Benny. "Oh, hi, Benny."

The man nodded. "Morning." Today, there was no easy-going smile. "You enjoy yourself last night?"

"I did. It was so much fun on the beach. You have a great family."

Benny nodded. "I also know my cousin didn't make it to his own bed last night."

She stayed quiet. That was between her and Sawyer.

Sawyer's cousin sighed. "Look, Sawyer's had a rough few years. He was in the military—"

"I know. He told me."

Benny paused. "He did?"

She nodded.

"He doesn't talk about it much."

"I get that it was tough for him. As was returning to civilian life."

Benny's brow creased. "He doesn't sleep well, and has nightmares."

Her stomach lurched. She'd had a taste of that herself the last few weeks, but being unable to sleep for *years*... Her heart squeezed for Sawyer.

She reached out and touched Benny's arm. "He credits this place, and you and your wife's family, for saving him."

Benny's gaze narrowed as he studied her face. "I was going to warn you off him. I don't want him hurt. But maybe you're not the selfish actress looking for a fling like I thought you were."

"I'm just a woman, Benny. And I wasn't looking for Sawyer, either, but he sure is hard to ignore. I don't get to meet many real, genuine guys like him."

Now, his cousin grinned. "Okay, I'm not going to pull the protective cousin routine."

She smiled back. "Good."

"Let's do dinner soon. My wife is an excellent cook. I'll call Sawyer to tee it up."

"That sounds great."

Hollis was still smiling as she headed down the sidewalk. She made a stop at the grocery store, and got the things she needed for dinner. She noted that some shelves were empty, with a small sign saying that the shipment was late. She guessed there were some challenges to living in paradise, if paradise was an island in the middle of the Pacific Ocean.

She carried her bags back to her car. The sun was warm, and she couldn't wait to go for a swim later.

"Oh my God!" a voice screeched.

Hollis almost dropped her bags. She turned and saw a young woman in tiny shorts and a blue bikini top aiming a phone at her. Everything about the woman screamed tourist. She had long, blonde hair, and the young man with her stood beside a red jeep with surfboards strapped to the top.

"You're Hollis Stanton! I can't believe it." The

THE HERO SHE DESERVES

woman turned, trying to get a selfie with herself and Hollis in the shot.

"No photos, please."

The woman ignored her.

Hollis turned away. "Have a great day."

"Oh my God, I just saw Hollis Stanton."

"I saw, babe," the man said. "Cool."

Without looking back, Hollis slid into her car. She pulled out as fast as she safely could, her hands flexing on the steering wheel.

She loved her fans, when they showed some respect and treated her like a person. Not when they were so focused on their own experience that they treated her like a zoo exhibit. She blew out a breath.

They were just some tourists passing through. It would be fine.

When she reached the house, she pulled up out front, and fished her phone out of her bag. One quick search and she closed her eyes, her head thudding back against the headrest.

The woman had already posted it on social media.

Just saw Hollis Stanton on Maui. #celebspotting #spotted #viral

Ugh. Okay, so Hollis had known she couldn't lay low forever, but she'd hoped it could last at least a week.

Gathering up the shopping bags, she headed inside. She put the groceries away. So, she'd been spotted. No one knew exactly where she was staying. It would be fine.

She changed into her favorite green bikini, then gathered up some scripts, and headed outside. Sitting by the pool, she lay on one of the pool loungers, spread on some sunscreen, and got reading.

Unfortunately, these scripts weren't as good as the other ones she'd read. She shot some texts off to Tave with her comments. Her rumbling stomach sent her to the kitchen to make a sandwich for lunch. As she ate, she wondered what Sawyer was doing. Her lips curled. He'd be in his uniform, looking all competent and official. No doubt some pretty tourists in bikinis would be drooling all over him. Now, she frowned. Okay, she didn't like that bit so much.

After lunch and some more reading, she finally decided it was time to hit the beach. She pulled on a white cover-up, slipped on her flip-flops, and grabbed a towel.

There were a handful of people spaced out along the beach. She carefully found a spot that wasn't too close to anyone. There were no windsurfers today; she guessed it wasn't windy enough.

She left her things on the sand, stripped off her cover-up, then walked down to the water. A feeling of peace washed over her, and she glanced up at the blue sky. She dipped her toes in the water, thrilled at the lovely, warm temperature. She waded farther out, then she dived into the water.

She swam a little, but didn't go too far out. She had a healthy fear of sharks. She bobbed in the gentle waves, and thought of Sawyer again.

Maybe they could come down for a moonlight swim? Or they could skinny-dip in the pool. She shivered, tingles flaring to life everywhere across her body. She couldn't wait to see him again.

Hopefully it wouldn't be much longer before he finished work. Maybe he'd still be in his uniform. Another shiver.

Hollis headed back toward the shore.

Out of the corner of her eye, she saw a dark shape in the water come nearer.

Instant fear shot through her. Then a man in a snorkeling mask rose out of the water.

She gasped, relief hitting her. Not a shark. He was wearing a black wetsuit.

"Hi." She pressed a palm to her chest. "You scared me."

He didn't respond, just lunged for her.

He grabbed the back of her neck and her arm.

Adrenaline punched through her system. "Hey, hands off, asshole!"

He still didn't say anything.

Then he dragged her back into deeper water and shoved her forward.

Hollis threw her arms out, water splashing. She was off balance and fell to her knees, the water up to her chest.

"What the hell? Let me go!"

Then the man shoved her head under the water.

Fear roared through her, and she tasted acid in her mouth. She thrashed, trying to break his hold.

But he was bigger and stronger.

She fought, bubbles churning through the water.

God, he was trying to *kill* her.

CHAPTER EIGHT

"So two iPads, a cellphone, and your wallet?"

"Yes." The upset woman pressed her hands to her sunburned cheeks. "This is *not* what we wanted on our dream Maui holiday."

The woman's husband wrapped an arm around her. "We thought there was no crime on Maui."

Sawyer continued taking notes. "The crime rate is low, but unfortunately, with so many tourists visiting the island every year, we do have some crime. Most of it is petty theft." Especially when tourists like these left their valuables in plain sight on their car seat while they swam at the beach. "Mrs. Elden, we'll do what we can to track down your things. In the meantime, I suggest you contact your bank and cancel your credit cards."

"So much stress." She pulled a face.

Sawyer looked at his notes. "You're staying in Kapalua, right? Do you know Merriman's?"

Mr. Elden nodded. "We heard the restaurant has great food and a stunning location right on Kapalua Bay."

"I know the chef there," Sawyer said. "Make a reservation for tonight, and I'll tell him to expect you. He'll take good care of you and help you forget this unpleasantness."

Mrs. Elden gave him a watery smile. "That sounds great."

Her husband nodded. "We'll do that. Thanks, Deputy Lane."

"My pleasure. And please, keep any valuables out of sight. Better to lock them in the trunk."

The couple headed back to their car, while Sawyer climbed into his SUV.

It had been a relatively quiet day at work. His main task had been to help the Maui PD with a drug search. It didn't matter where you lived, drugs were always a problem. The day had dragged on, because all he could think about was Hollis, and when he'd see her again.

He picked up his radio. "This is Lane."

"Hi, Sawyer." Debbie, one of their dispatchers, answered.

"I'm finished with the car break in at Kanaha. I'm clocking off and heading home."

"Acknowledged. Enjoy your evening."

Soon, he was driving toward Hollis's place. He knew he should go home first to change, but he was too eager to see her.

He pulled up next to her car and knocked on the front door. There was no answer. He peered inside, but saw no sign of her. He circled the house. She wasn't in the pool, but he remembered she'd mentioned that she wanted to go down to the beach for a swim. He smiled. Maybe he'd get to see her in a bikini.

Memories of the bikini she wore last night—the one he'd torn off her—stirred.

He headed onto the sand, hands on his hips, and sunglasses on his face. He walked along, scanning for her.

He saw a guy in a wetsuit and snorkeling mask, but no Hollis. That's when he spotted her things—towel, flip flops.

He frowned and glanced at the water again. *Where was Hollis?*

That's when he realized the guy in the wetsuit looked wrong. He was tense, partly crouched and bent over.

The water churned in front of him.

Fuck. Sawyer's body tensed. He was holding someone down.

Hollis.

Sawyer ran, sprinting hard across the sand. "Hey!"

At his bellow, the man's head whipped up. Sawyer couldn't see much behind the mask.

"Let her go!"

The man dropped Hollis and sprinted out of the water. He ran down the beach away from Sawyer.

The soldier in him wanted to give chase, but Hollis was facedown in the water.

His brain stopped. He charged forward, splashing through knee-deep water to reach her. The next wave brought her closer and he grabbed her.

"Hollis!" He flipped her over.

She coughed.

Thank fuck. She coughed up more seawater, her hair sticking to her face. Her skin was pale.

"Baby." He lifted her into his arms, then jogged up onto the sand.

He dropped to his knees, holding her close. He looked around again and saw no sign of her attacker. His jaw tightened.

This is my island, asshole. I will find you.

He smoothed Hollis's hair back from her face. "Are you okay?"

She coughed again and nodded. Tiredly, she leaned against his chest. His uniform was wet, but he didn't give a shit.

Her hands twisted in the fabric. "I'm okay. Now." She made a small hiccupping sound. "Sawyer, that man —" Her voice cracked.

"He tried to drown you."

A sob escaped her.

"Shh, you're safe now." He wrapped his arms around her and held her close. He'd fucking do whatever he needed to do, in order to keep her that way.

He lifted her and rose. He stopped, bent down and grabbed her things, then headed up to the house. He set her on a pool lounger while he unlocked the door. She started shivering, despite the warm afternoon.

He lifted her again.

"I can walk," she said.

"I don't care."

He carried her inside and straight to her bedroom, then into her bathroom. He set her on the side of the huge tub while he started the shower running. He set the

81

temperature to hot. Archer's bathroom was three times the size of Sawyer's, with glossy cream tiles and giant shower with lots of showerheads.

"Come on, you're in shock. We need to get you warm." He helped her up, kicked his wet boots off, then stepped into the shower with her.

"Your uniform—"

"Will be fine." He gripped her arms and carefully checked her over. He could see bruises forming on her arms in the shape of the man's fingers. He locked down the rage burning inside him. "You should see a doctor."

"I'm okay, Sawyer. I promise. I stopped fighting him to try and get him to let me go. I never swallowed any water."

Seeing that man pushing her under... Sawyer ground his teeth together. He'd be seeing it in his head for a long time.

He tipped some shampoo into his hand and washed her hair. Then he pulled his wet clothes off, and wrung them out.

He felt her gaze on him. He was glad to see the shock and fear were wearing off.

When they got out, he wrapped a towel around his waist, then wrapped another around her. He dried her off.

"I have a bag with gym clothes in my SUV. I'll go and get it."

A flash of fear crossed her face before she hid it. He realized she was scared to be alone.

He grabbed her hand and squeezed. "I'll be right back. I promise."

When he returned, she was dressed in sleek, fitted pants and a light sweater.

Sawyer quickly changed. When he came back to the living room, she was on the couch, rubbing her arms. He sat down beside her. "You're safe now."

She swallowed and nodded. "I don't understand why someone would do this."

"Did you know the man who attacked you?"

"No. It was hard to see his face with the mask on, but I'm certain I'd never seen him before."

"Hollis, I need to call a fellow deputy. Get him to come out and take your statement."

Her mouth flattened.

"Jesse is a friend. He'll be discreet. He's not going to share with anyone that you're on the island."

She fiddled with her hair. With damp hair and her bare face, she looked so much younger.

"Hollis, he could attack and hurt somebody else."

A stricken look crossed her face." "Okay. Call your friend."

"Good." Sawyer squeezed her shoulder. "Then it's time for you to tell me who you're hiding from."

Her mouth firmed into a flat line, but she gave him a small nod.

STILL SHAKEN, Hollis tried to get warm. She listened to Sawyer's deep voice as he spoke on his cellphone.

If Sawyer hadn't arrived when he did...

A violent shiver wracked her.

"Here." Sawyer grabbed the throw blanket off the back of the couch and wrapped it around her. He sat down beside her.

"I'm fine," she tried to reassure him. "I know that I'm okay and safe. This is just some sort of delayed reaction."

"It's normal. You had a shock."

She twisted her hands together.

A second later, he hauled her onto his lap. She threw her arms around him and held on. God, he was so warm. She pressed her face to his strong neck. The warmth of his body seeped into her, and she breathed in his scent. He smelled like her shower gel, and she smiled.

A big hand stroked down her back. "I've got you."

It felt good leaning on someone. Having someone she could depend on. *Don't get used to it, Hols.*

"Jesse is on his way," Sawyer said. "He said he won't be long."

She nodded.

"Do you want something to drink? Tea? Whiskey?"

"No, I'm all right." She lifted her head and met his hazel eyes. "Thanks, Sawyer. For saving me."

His face darkened. "I'm just sorry I couldn't catch the bastard."

She cupped his bearded cheek.

"Now—" his face turned even more serious "—it's time you tell me what the hell's going on. My gut is telling me this wasn't a random attack."

Her stomach did a sickening twirl. "I need to...move." She pushed off his lap and paced across the room. She stared out the window, but for once, the view of the ocean didn't calm her.

"It started with a stupid party that I didn't even want to go to." She turned. Sawyer was sitting there, leaning forward, his hands dangling between his legs, his entire focus on her.

Had anyone ever looked at her like that before? Like he saw *her* and not the façade of Hollis Stanton, the actress.

"Go on," he urged.

She took a deep breath. "It was a party at the home of Michael Reuben. My agent said it would look bad to turn down an invite."

A groove appeared on Sawyer's brow. "Reuben. The movie producer?"

She nodded. "A powerful and important one. I don't really like him."

"Why?"

"No solid reason. He just gives me the creeps."

"So what happened at his party?"

"I was looking for the powder room and got lost. Down the hall, I could hear him talking with a man. They were talking about shipments and sanctions. I only heard snatches, and then they spoke in Russian."

"Shipments of what?"

She shrugged a shoulder. "I didn't hear."

"Is Reuben Russian?"

"No, he's from California, but I don't really know his family history."

"There are lots of sanctions on Russia at the moment, so any sort of shipments would be illegal."

She bit her lip. "I know."

"What happened next?"

"Reuben's bodyguard heard me and came out. Reuben followed, and I acted tipsy and like I hadn't heard anything."

"Did you see the other man? The one Reuben was talking with?

"I didn't. I hightailed it out of there." She pressed a hand to her chest.

"That's not the end of it," Sawyer said.

She gave a harsh laugh. "No. I didn't know what to do. I didn't have much information, so I didn't go to the police. What could I say? I heard some people speak in Russian and mention sanctions? But then over the next week, I felt like someone was watching me anytime I was out in public." She released a breath. "That's not unusual, though. People recognize me."

"Go on."

"Then, there was a car crash."

Sawyer cursed. "Were you hurt?"

"No, just shaken. A black SUV crashed into me. They didn't stop. Just drove off. The police said the car was stolen." She looked down at the floor. "Then I found a camera...in my bedroom."

"Jesus." He rose.

"I freaked out. I felt like I was losing my mind." She closed her eyes for a second. "Someone was either toying with me, or I was going crazy."

Sawyer cupped her shoulders. "Your mind is fine, Hollis. I like it a lot."

She shot him a small smile. "Oh, is that what you like about me?"

"Among other things." His rugged face turned serious again. "You came to Maui to hide."

"Yes. I guess I hoped things would blow over. I guess I was wrong. Are you sure it wasn't just a random attacker?"

"It's not likely. That kind of thing doesn't happen around here much, and he didn't look random."

Her shoulders sagged.

"Has anything else worried you since you've been here?"

"Apart from the hiking trail? No. *Wait.* My favorite silver bracelet, a gift from my stepdad, and a bottle of perfume are missing. I can't find them anywhere."

He stiffened. "Missing from the house?"

Nausea swelled inside her. "Yes. From my bedroom."

His next curse was very creative.

"I also thought someone was watching me in Paia today, but then I ran into Benny. He was going to warn the nasty actress away from his cousin, but I think he likes me."

Sawyer grunted. "Benny needs to mind his own business."

"I thought the sensation of being watched must have been him, or the pesky tourists who snapped some pics of me." She pulled a face. "They posted them online, by the way."

"And a few hours later someone tries to kill you."

Oh, shit. That was bad.

"All these little things, and now someone tried to drown you." He shook his head. "I don't like it."

Hollis felt cold again, like she'd stepped into a

freezer. She walked toward him, and he pulled her close. She pressed her cheek to his chest, and heard the steady, solid beat of his heart.

Trust him. Hippie Lavender's voice echoed in her head.

The rumble of a car's engine came from outside. She stiffened.

"That'll be Jesse. Don't mention Reuben. Just give Jess the details of today's attack. I need to think about this some more." His gaze narrowed. "And I definitely need more intel on Michael Reuben."

CHAPTER NINE

"The steaks are almost ready," Sawyer called out, as he flipped the steaks on the grill by the pool. Inside, Hollis was making a salad.

He watched her through the glass as she waved at him. She was standing at the kitchen island, and was quiet, edgy, and off-balance. She hadn't been able to sit still while she'd been giving Jesse a rundown on the attack.

Sawyer felt a hard shot of anger. They didn't know if the asshole who'd tried to kill her was still on the island, but Sawyer would find him.

He pulled out his cellphone and texted Jesse.

You get anything on this guy, you let me know straight away.

Jesse responded immediately.

You know I will, Sawyer. I've passed his description onto Maui PD.

But Sawyer heard what Jesse didn't say. They didn't have much to go on.

Thanks again for coming out.

Next, Sawyer made a call.

"Sawyer?" Vander's deep voice answered. "Everything okay?"

"I need some help."

"Whatever you need, you've got it."

Vander owned one of the best security firms in the country. If anyone could help him, it was Vander. "I met someone. A woman."

"Really? So you did listen to my advice."

Sawyer turned his back to the sliding glass doors. "She's not from here, it's just a temporary thing."

"Okay."

"But she's in danger. Someone attacked her at the beach today, and tried to drown her."

Vander cursed. "Is she okay?"

"Yes, although she's shaken." As was Sawyer.

"I'm guessing this wasn't random?"

"Not a chance."

"What's her name?"

Sawyer prodded the steaks again. "Hollis. Hollis Stanton."

There was a long pause. "She has the same name as the actress?"

"No, she is the actress."

Vander whistled. "When I told you to find a woman, you didn't mess around."

"She's staying in a holiday house near mine. Vander, someone's after her."

"A stalker?"

"No. I need you to dig into a man called Michael Reuben."

Another pause. "The wealthy Hollywood producer. I'll get Ace on it."

Sawyer told Vander what Hollis had overheard at Reuben's house.

"Hell, it sounds like she stumbled onto something nasty," Vander mused.

"I'm *not* letting her get hurt." Sawyer turned, and let his gaze drift back to her through the glass.

"All right. Let me do some digging. I'll call you when I've got something. Do you need backup?"

"Not yet, but I'll keep it in mind. Thanks, Vander."

"Always."

After he slipped his cellphone back in his pocket, he put the steaks on a plate. He headed inside.

"I was going to cook for you tonight." Hollis's nose wrinkled. "My famous pepper steak stir fry. Instead, you worked all day, had to deal with my drama, and then had to cook the steaks."

He set the plate on the island. "Hey." He cupped her cheeks. "Getting attacked wasn't your fault. And keeping you safe is no hardship."

She swallowed. "You're the real deal, aren't you?"

He cocked a brow.

She pressed her hands to his chest. "A good guy."

He stroked a thumb over her lip. "I'm not a saint."

She smiled. "Oh, I know." She nipped his thumb. "Come on, let's eat before the steaks get cold."

They sat at the table, with a moonlit view of the

ocean beyond the pool. After a little while, Hollis relaxed, talking about the scripts she'd been reading, and which ones she'd liked. But after they'd cleaned up and washed the dishes, that edgy tension leaked back in again.

He could tell she was anxious and exhausted.

"Go and get ready for bed. I'll lock up."

"You're staying?" She didn't hide the hope in her voice.

"Of course, I'm staying."

With a relieved nod, she disappeared into the bedroom.

Sawyer checked all the doors and windows. He scanned out back, taking in the shadows under the trees. Was someone out there? Watching her place?

Bring it. They'd have to go through him first to get to her.

Back in the bedroom, he found Hollis in a short, sexy nightgown, in a shade of blue-gray that suited her. His cock twitched.

Down boy. She was tired and vulnerable. Tonight was about taking care of her, and making sure she got some sleep.

He pulled off his shirt, and her gaze zeroed in on his chest.

"Get into bed, Hollis. You're tired."

He headed for the bathroom and brushed his teeth. Back in the bedroom, he set his SIG Sauer handgun down on the bedside table.

"I'm not sure I can sleep." She was under the covers and propped up on the pillows.

"You'll sleep."

"You can't just order me to sleep, Sawyer."

He climbed in, and hauled her close, then pressed a kiss to her mouth. Then he lay back, pulled her face to his neck.

With a sigh, she relaxed against him. "I'm glad you're here."

Those quiet words arrowed into him, and hooked in deep. He'd avoided strong connections for a long time. Hell, it wasn't that he'd avoided people, he just hadn't been capable.

Old screams, the scent of fire. He closed his eyes, then opened them again. But with Hollis, it was so easy.

He stroked her hair. "There's nowhere else I'd rather be." Then he leaned over and grabbed the remote for the TV attached to the bedroom wall.

As he flicked through Archer's streaming services, he finally found what he was looking for. *The Wizard of Oz* came on.

Hollis made a sound. "Sawyer..."

"Just relax, gorgeous."

She snuggled deeper against him. "Watching movies is my escape. It always was. That's why I love acting. I always hope I can give my fans the same escape. The same chance to just put their crappy day behind them."

He kept stroking her hair, watching the light from the show flicker over her beautiful face. He wanted her to stop thinking about her crappy day.

He wasn't sure how much time had passed, but Dorothy was having her adventure along the yellow brick road. He looked down and realized that Hollis was asleep, her hand pressed against his chest.

I'll keep you safe, gorgeous.

SAWYER CAME AWAKE IN AN INSTANT. Just like when he'd been in Ghost Ops.

He stilled, staring at the ceiling. His internal body clock told him it was one or two o'clock in the morning.

Hell, he'd fallen asleep and slept soundly for several hours. That hadn't happened in...he couldn't remember how long. Hollis was curled against his side, fast asleep and breathing softly.

What had woken him?

He carefully slid from the bed and grabbed his SIG. The metal was cool against his fingers. Silently, he moved through the house. He knew how to move without being seen or heard.

He scanned the living area. Nothing. Just shadows dancing in the darkness.

There. A darker, bigger shadow at the sliding doors. He tensed.

Sticking to the wall, he moved closer. He couldn't make out any details, because it was too dark.

Again. Definite movement by the pool.

Sawyer reached out and flicked on the outside light.

The dark shape of a man raced for the trees, moving fast. He disappeared.

Fuck. More than anything, Sawyer wanted to go out there and give chase. Run the fucker down and stop him. But he couldn't leave Hollis alone and unprotected.

He left the lights on and circled through the house, checking the locks on the doors and windows.

Finally, he slipped back into bed, keeping his gun in easy reach. Hollis made a sleepy sound and rolled into his body, then relaxed.

"No one's going to hurt you." He slid his hand to her hip.

Then he stared at the ceiling. He wouldn't sleep. He'd make sure their visitor didn't return.

HOLLIS SNUGGLED INTO THE PILLOW, drowsily wondering if she needed to get up and go to work. What movie was she filming at the moment?

The pillow shifted, and she realized it was actually a firm arm.

Oh.

Her eyes blinked open. Sunlight was coming in through the gap in the curtains. And Sawyer Lane was in her bed.

Now *that* was a sight she could easily wake up to every day.

"Morning." His voice was a deep rumble. "Did you sleep all right?"

"I slept really well, considering." She smiled. "The best sleep I've had in a while."

"Good."

"You?"

"I don't usually need a lot of sleep, but I got a solid few hours."

Something in his voice made her cock her head. He sounded slightly surprised.

"I'm glad." Then her full bladder demanded attention. "I'll be back." She slipped out of the bed and hurried to the bathroom.

When she came back, her mouth was minty fresh. Sawyer was sitting up in the bed, his chest on display.

She *really* liked his chest.

In the clear light of day, her gaze drifted to a circular scar on his shoulder—it had to be from a bullet. It made her wonder about everything he'd been through.

"I'm glad you stayed, even if the night was quiet."

His jaw tightened and he swung his legs off the bed.

Her stomach did a nasty swoop. "It was quiet, right?"

"We had a nocturnal visitor. Don't worry. I scared him off."

God. Someone had come here. To her house. A mix of fear, anger, and despair hit her like a bucket of cold water to the face.

She stumbled back a step. "I should leave. Go...somewhere."

"Fuck, no." He reached for her hand and pulled her onto the bed. She rested on her knees beside him.

"You go, he might find you again. And you'd be unprotected. You stay here, where I can protect you."

"This isn't your problem, Sawyer."

He cupped her jaw. "It is now."

"Sawyer..."

"I called an old military friend last night. He runs a

security company in San Francisco. He's going to look into Reuben."

A rush of more emotions filled her. "You believe me? That this has something to do with him?"

"Yeah. I do."

It made her feel that she wasn't so alone.

"My friend will also see if anyone connected to Reuben is on the island. And I'll be here with you."

"Thank you."

"I don't want any thanks."

"I'm tired of being confused and afraid." She gripped his hand tighter. It was big, solid. "I'm *not* letting Reuben, or any of his goons, push me around."

Sawyer gave her a half smile. "Good."

Suddenly, she needed him. She wanted something good right now. She wanted to drown out the fear and helplessness with something else.

Something she chose, that she controlled.

She walked closer on her knees, then straddled him. Heat pumped off him. "I'm not letting *anyone* push me around. I want to make my own decisions. Do what I want."

His hands gripped her hips. "And what do you want, gorgeous?"

"You."

She kissed him. It was aggressive and filled with need. She bit his lip.

His hands slid around to cup her ass, squeezed. "Take whatever you need, Hollis."

Her heartbeat picked up. She kissed him again, undulating on the hard cock growing beneath her.

He pushed down one strap of her nightgown and bared her breast. He made a hungry sound and pulled her closer. His mouth closed over her nipple, tugging hard.

"*Sawyer.*" She speared her hands into his hair. "I can't wait any longer. I need you inside me."

"You're the boss. You're in charge here. You want my cock, take it."

A spurt of giddy pleasure filled her.

She shifted back and looked at the fabric of his boxer shorts stretched over his cock. She pushed the fabric out of the way and freed him. She took his solid cock in both hands and stroked.

He groaned. She was wet, aching between her legs.

"Look at you. Gorgeous red hair, sexy nightgown, desire in your eyes. Fucking perfect."

She ran a thumb over the swollen head of his cock and found it slick with pre-come. His deep groan sent a thrill through her. She couldn't wait any longer.

"I need you, Sawyer." Hollis rose up, positioned him, and then sank down. With one firm thrust of her hips, she took him deep. Her moan mixed with his curse.

His fingers bunched in her nightgown. "Look at you taking me." His gaze was locked between her thighs.

"Sawyer..." She started to ride him.

"That what you needed? My cock?"

"*Yes.*" The pleasure was building fast. She picked up speed, riding him hard.

"That's my cock filling you." His fingers bit into her ass.

A part of her hoped he left some bruises, that he marked her.

Then his mouth was on hers, driving the desire higher. She felt him nudge a hand between her thighs, and then his thumb was on her clit. She gripped his shoulders and met his fierce gaze.

"Fucking perfect," he growled again.

On the next thrust, Hollis's orgasm ripped through her. She threw her head back and cried out his name.

His low growl followed as he found his own release. "*Fuck. Hollis.*"

CHAPTER TEN

He liked watching Hollis putter in the kitchen, cooking breakfast. Today she was wearing denim shorts, with a white button-down shirt, and her red hair in a messy bun. He really liked seeing her like this.

Sawyer didn't see an actress. He saw a beautiful, smart, warm woman.

"My world-famous scrambled eggs." Holding the frypan, she served the eggs onto plates on the island.

He sipped his juice. "World-famous, huh?"

She grinned. "Yes. Everything I make is world-famous."

He pulled her close and kissed her. She instantly melted into him and kissed him back.

He kept it gentle. The sex this morning had been amazing, but it had also been fast and rough. Now he just wanted to savor her.

They sat at the table, and he tried a forkful of eggs. "These are great."

"It's my secret ingredient. I'll never tell, even to you, Deputy Lane."

"I could get it out of you."

She shot him a look. "You probably could, but it would take time, and you have to get to work."

He cleared his throat. "No, I don't."

She paused with her fork in the air. "I thought you did."

"I called my boss while you were in the shower and asked for a few days off."

She stared at him. "To stay with me?"

He nodded. He sure as hell wasn't leaving her alone and defenseless.

"Sawyer..." She blew out a breath. "I'll pay you."

His jaw tightened. "I don't want your money, Hollis. I want to keep you safe."

She eyed him. "Because that's what you do."

"It is, and I'm good at it." He grabbed her hand. "But also because I don't want anything to happen to you."

Things worked through her eyes. "All right. Thank you."

He leaned over and kissed her on the nose. "Good."

"When do you think you'll hear from your friend? About Reuben."

"Today. Vander doesn't fuck around."

"Wait?" She set her fork down. "Vander? Vander Norcross?"

Sawyer raised a brow. "You know him?"

"I've heard of him. I know several celebrities who've thrown lots of money at him to come and do bodyguard work for them. Which he refuses to do. One of his guys,

Rome Nash, did protection for a friend of mine." Hollis cocked her head. "How do you know Vander?"

"We worked together in the military."

Her gaze narrowed. "You were a SEAL. In the Navy. Vander was Army. I heard that he was in Delta Force, then some shadowy, top-secret team."

Sawyer made a noncommittal sound.

"Wow. You were on that team, as well. I knew you were a badass, but…"

He tugged on her hair. "Eat your eggs."

They were almost finished when there was the sound of a car out front. Hollis tensed.

"It's okay," Sawyer said. "I called out our fingerprint tech to print the back door. We might get lucky and get a hit."

"You have a fingerprint technician on Maui?"

"Well, Leilani is sort of a Jill-of-all-trades."

There was a knock at the front door.

Sawyer crossed the room and opened it. "Leilani."

"Big guy." The small woman pushed inside. "I *love* this place."

Today, her shirt was bright blue, and her trousers were multi-colored with splotches of orange, red, blue, and white.

Leilani stopped suddenly, staring at Hollis. "Oh my God."

Sawyer took a step forward. "Leilani—"

She whirled and pointed at him. "You got laid. *Finally.*"

He looked at the ceiling. *Jesus.*

"Hi, I'm Leilani Sola." She held a hand out to Hollis and they shook.

"Hi, I'm—"

"Hollis Stanton," Leilani finished with a no-nonsense tone. "I'm more of an action-movie fan, myself. So, if you could star in one of those, I'll watch more of your movies." She looked around. "This place is so awesome."

"Thanks for coming, Leilani," Sawyer said.

"No problem. Where do you need me, big guy?"

"Sliding door at the back. To the pool. We had an intruder last night."

"On it." Leilani glanced at the kitchen. "Any chance I can get some of those eggs? They smell great, and I missed breakfast."

Hollis blinked. "Sure. I'll cook some up for you."

Sawyer shook his head. Only Leilani would have no hesitation in asking Hollywood's most in demand actress to cook her breakfast. He watched her open her bag, then dust and take prints from the door. Then, she set up her laptop and portable scanner on the island. Her fingers flew as she tapped away.

"You get any decent prints?"

"I did. I'll rule out yours and Hollis's but there was a nice, juicy one I feel good about."

"You're pretty comfortable with computers." Hollis pushed a plate of eggs across to the young woman.

"Yeah. I do crime scene collection, IT work, some admin. Whatever we need done around the office."

Sawyer crossed his arms. "Leilani is good at everything. She keeps the office ticking over."

"And the big guy here gets to crack heads and snap handcuffs on bad guys."

"I don't crack heads... Often."

"True. One look at you and the misbehaving male tourists shake in their flip-flops and awful Hawaiian shirts." Leilani grinned. "The female ones drool and want to climb him."

Sawyer made an annoyed sound.

"Isn't he cute when he gets embarrassed?" Leilani teased.

Hollis smiled. "He is."

"Don't encourage her," he warned.

Leilani's computer pinged. "Ooh, we've got something." She frowned. "That's weird."

"What?" Sawyer asked, looking over her shoulder.

"There's a hit, but no name. Looks like it's linked to a couple of Interpol cases."

Interpol? What the hell did that mean?

"Want me to request access?" Leilani asked.

He knew that that would take too long. "No. Can you email me the print?"

"Sure thing."

Vander's team would be quicker.

"You going to ask Vander?" Leilani said.

"No comment. Thanks for coming, Leilani."

"You bet." She packed up her stuff. "Thanks for the eggs, Hollywood."

Hollis's lips twitched. "You're welcome, Hawaii."

Leilani grinned. "I like her. Enjoy your days off, big guy. Keep your girl safe. Nice to meet you, Hollis."

"Nice to meet you, too.

Leilani nodded. "And you keep him safe back." She waved as she sailed out the door. "Bye."

———

HOLLIS FOLLOWED Sawyer into Island Brew. The scent of coffee hit her and she instantly felt better.

Koa looked at them, eyes widening. "Oh, you two are—"

"Getting a coffee." Kiana elbowed her brother. "I'll make you both something special."

"Thanks," Hollis replied.

Sawyer pressed his hand to her lower back, and she felt tingles spread over her skin. She'd never felt like this before. She was so aware of him. It wasn't just his looks and body, it was him taking care of her.

No one did that. Her mom hadn't. Hollis had been taking care of herself for a long time.

Her cellphone rang and she saw Tave's name. She pressed it to her ear. "Hey, you don't have to check up on me all the time." She mouthed "it's my agent" to Sawyer.

"Hollis."

Tave rarely called her by her full name. Her stomach tightened. "What's wrong?"

Sawyer leaned closer, shoulders tensing.

"It's all over the news that you're on Hawaii, specifically Maui. The vultures will be gunning for pics of you. Preferably in a bikini with some cellulite, or locking lips with a toy boy fling."

She closed her eyes. "Okay." Her voice was dull.

"Just wanted to give you a heads up."

"All right."

"You okay?"

She dragged in a breath. "Someone attacked me on the beach yesterday." She didn't share the gory details. She didn't want Tave to worry, and the man could be a champion worrier.

"*What?* Are you all right?"

"I'm fine. Sawyer saved me."

"Is Deputy Hottie with you right now?" Tave's voice held an edge.

She met Sawyer's green-gold eyes. "He is."

"Put him on."

"What?"

"Put him on the phone, Red."

She huffed out a breath and held the phone out to Sawyer. "My overprotective, bossy agent wants to talk with you."

Sawyer took the phone and turned away. "Sawyer Lane." He was quiet for a moment. "Yeah. Did you?" Another pause. "She's all right, and I'll be making sure she stays that way." A muscle ticked in his jaw. "I don't want payment. I'm not on her fucking payroll. Yeah, all right, Hall. I'll keep you updated."

Hollis crossed her arms. "Are the big, strong men finished taking care of the silly, little woman?"

"He was worried. Just wanted to make sure you aren't alone."

Her shoulders sagged.

"Here you go." Kiana handed a coffee over. "Looks

106

like you need it. A pistachio latte for our lovely tourist. And for our deputy, a dark chocolate mocha."

Sawyer gave the twins a chin lift.

"Hey, you two," Hollis said. "You'll hear about this soon anyway, and probably have people in here asking, but my name isn't really Holli."

Kiana waved a hand "It's Hollis Stanton."

Hollis's mouth dropped open.

Koa nodded. "We knew the first day you came in here. *The Princess Affair* is my favorite movie. I knew who you were straight away."

He named the teen hit that had given her the big break in her career.

"I liked *The Princess Affair* 2 better," Kiana said. "That guy who played the prince was hot."

"You knew." They hadn't let on. Hadn't treated her differently.

Kiana shrugged. "We guessed you were trying to keep it quiet that you were here. We understood."

Throat tight, she nodded. "Thanks."

"Dad made walnut brownies today." Koa gestured to the plate of baked treats on the counter. "He was in a nutty mood. I think we all need one."

"Hmm." Hollis took a bite. "Delicious."

Koa leaned forward, resting his elbows on the counter. "So, do you two have plans?"

"Just coffee and shopping," Hollis said.

"You should come to Mama's tonight. Both of you. We have family over from the Big Island and we're having dinner. More the merrier."

"Mama's?" Hollis asked.

"Paia's best restaurant," Sawyer said.

"*Maui's* best restaurant," Koa countered.

"Mama's Fish House is an institution," Kiana said. "Amazing seafood using Hawaiian and Polynesian cooking techniques."

"And a great location," Koa added.

"That sounds wonderful." Hollis gripped her drink tighter. "But I'm guessing there will be lots of people there, and now the secret's out that I'm here, there might be paparazzi and people trying to take photos."

Koa made a scoffing sound. "We'll warn our family, they won't mind. And Mama's always has a table for us away from the main area."

She glanced at Sawyer.

"Would be a tragedy to miss the food at Mama's." He slid an arm around her. "I'll make sure no one bothers you."

Her heart tightened. She nodded at the twins. "We'll be there."

They waved their goodbyes and headed back onto the sidewalk.

"Is it safe to go to dinner?" she asked. "The guy from the beach—"

"We'll be in a crowd, in a public place." He touched her cheek. "And I'll be with you."

Now her chest loosened, warmth welling inside her.

"Come on, I need to pick something up." He headed down the street, tugging on her hand.

Hollis found herself looking around anxiously, wondering if her would-be killer was watching her, or some photographer was going to shove a lens in her face.

"Here." Sawyer opened the door to a store. The sign just said *Ken's*. The shelves were laden with appliances, computers, and gadgets, and the walls were covered with signs advertising just about everything. The air-conditioning was cranked up high, and chilled her skin.

"Sawyer, my man." The short, lean shopkeeper had Japanese heritage and beamed at Sawyer. "I've got what you wanted."

The man disappeared into the back, then returned, carrying a large box.

"What is it?" Hollis asked.

"A surprise." Sawyer pulled out a credit card and paid. "Thanks, Ken."

After that, they wandered back to Sawyer's SUV.

"It's nice to feel...normal," she told him. "No fans wanting selfies or autographs."

"It must get crazy."

"Yes, it does. People can be really weird sometimes." She looked around. "This is really nice."

"There she is!" a man yelled.

Sawyer's head whipped around, and Hollis looked over her shoulder. She spotted the man with the camera and huge lens instantly.

"Hollis, over here."

Another man with a camera stood across the street.

"Who's the guy?" the first man yelled.

"Come on." Sawyer urged her in front of him. "Get to my SUV."

Hollis picked up speed, frustration chewing at her. Nothing good ever lasted.

A crowd of tourists stood ahead on the sidewalk,

phones up and aimed her way. Ugh, she hated people sometimes.

Sawyer scowled at them. Hollis just focused on getting to the vehicle. When she saw the SUV, relief punched through her.

Yanking the back door open, Sawyer quickly shoved the box on the back seat. "Get in. Keep your head down."

Hollis didn't argue. She slid into the passenger seat. She just wanted to get out of there.

A moment later, Sawyer drove out onto the street and gunned the engine.

She leaned her head back against the seat and closed her eyes. "I knew it was coming. I guess I just hoped I had a few more days."

"I'll call Jesse. Get him to keep an eye on the photogs." His voice was a low growl. "If they step out of line, it'll be my pleasure to boot them off the island."

She clenched her hands together. "It won't take them long to find out I'm staying at Archer's house."

"I'm taking the long way home. I'll make sure no one is following us." He reached over and squeezed her knee. "I'm not letting *anyone* near you. Photographers, or attackers."

There he went, making her heart go crazy again. Hollis's cellphone rang. She pulled it out and groaned.

"Problem?" he asked.

"My mother." She dragged in a deep breath. "Hi, Mom."

"Hollis." Kate Charles always had a strident note to her voice, and was always in a rush. "You haven't called in almost two weeks."

"I've been busy."

"Playacting. I'm sure you could've found some time."

Hollis sighed. "I've actually taken some time off."

"Really? You don't really have set hours. Do you need a vacation? I worked two jobs when you were little, and I didn't get any time off."

She felt a headache spring to life. "My job often requires long hours, Mom." She rubbed the groove forming between her eyes. She knew explaining things wasn't worth the effort. "Anyway, how are you?" It was always best to turn the conversation onto her mother.

"I'm dating a lovely man." Her mom's voice warmed. "He's a doctor. A skin specialist. He works so hard."

Her mother rattled on about her new man, and only needed a few murmurs of agreement from Hollis.

"That's great, Mom. I'm glad you're happy."

"Hollis..." Her mom paused. "I hate to ask, but my allowance ran dry early this month. I needed some new clothes."

Hollis provided a condo and monthly allowance for her mother. Thankfully, she didn't often overspend. She might not like Hollis being an actress, but she certainly liked the benefits. That said, her mother always hated asking for money.

"I'll transfer some more money into your account."

"Thank you," her mom said quietly.

"Look, I need to go. I'll call you again soon."

"Yes, all right. I need to get to an appointment. Good-bye, Hollis."

"Bye, Mom." She ended the call and stifled a sigh.

"You didn't tell your mom about what's happening?" Sawyer asked.

She glanced over at him. "No. I don't want to involve her. She'll blame me for choosing such a frivolous profession. Mom didn't think I needed a vacation from my 'playacting.'" Old bitterness welled.

"She should be proud of you. Of everything you've achieved. And she definitely should be worried about you."

"She...doesn't have it in her." Hollis lifted her chin. "Besides, I'm proud of myself, and worried about myself, too."

He reached over and took her hand. "You're not alone."

Her heart skipped a beat.

They arrived at her house and Sawyer carried the box inside.

The curiosity was killing her. "What is it?"

"It's a gift for you."

"Really?" Delight filled her. She often got trinkets and gift bags when she attended functions, but they were never personalized gifts. Tave always got her a gift card for her favorite day spa for her birthday and Christmas.

She opened the box and looked inside. It was a new coffee machine.

"Oh." She grinned as she pulled it out.

"So you can get your caffeine hit a bit sooner. Well, I guess this gift is actually for Archer, but I got it for you."

She was so touched. "Thank you." She rose up on her toes and pressed a kiss to his cheek.

His arm circled her waist and squeezed. "You've got

time to make a cup before we need to get ready to go to Mama's."

She nipped at his lips. "I can think of a better way to fill the time."

His arm tightened. "I like the way you think, Ms. Stanton."

CHAPTER ELEVEN

Sawyer led Hollis toward Mama's.

The charming building was nestled in a grove of palm trees, right on a picturesque beach. A hand-carved sign over the door said *Mama's*.

"This is so nice," she said.

He was barely looking at the restaurant. He couldn't take his gaze off Hollis. She was wearing a slinky, green dress that was perfect for her coloring. The fabric slithered over her body, and the deep *V* showed off her cleavage, while the hem ended at mid-thigh, showcasing slim legs.

Gorgeous.

"Sawyer?"

She was looking at him expectantly.

"People probably tell you how beautiful you are all the time."

"I don't care about people. They say horrible things about me, too. They love to post pictures of me leaving the gym with no makeup, or mid-run showing off some cellulite." She tossed her hair back.

"You're beautiful."

Her lips quirked. "Thank you."

"Come on." Just as he took her hand, his cellphone rang. He pulled it out and stilled. "It's Vander."

She bit her lip and nodded.

"Vander," Sawyer said.

"Hi, Sawyer." Vander's tone was unhappy.

"You found something."

"Not enough to get the full picture. My team are discreetly digging, as we don't want to tip him off, but from what we can tell, Michael Reuben is not a nice guy. He's got his fingers in plenty of shady dealings."

"Not surprised," Sawyer muttered.

"We haven't uncovered anything on the shipments Hollis heard him mention yet, or the Russian link, but his business dealings are definitely not legal."

Sawyer released a breath. "Okay, thanks. You'll keep on it?"

"You know it. You just focus on Hollis."

His hand tightened on hers, their fingers entwining. That, he had no trouble doing.

As he slid the phone away, she watched him, worry in her eyes.

"That was Vander with an update. Nothing much to report yet, but it looks like Reuben has plenty of shady business dealings."

She glanced away, and he knew she wasn't taking in the view.

Sawyer squeezed her fingers. "Vander will keep digging. I'm going to keep you safe."

"Thanks, Sawyer."

"For tonight, I want you to not think of it. Just enjoy the good food and good company."

She pasted on a smile, but he could tell it wasn't real. He'd get her there. He'd make it his goal for the night.

He pulled her inside.

"Welcome, Sawyer," the young, handsome host said, with a smile. "The Makana family said you were joining them."

"Thanks, Luke." Sawyer ignored the starstruck look the young man shot at Hollis.

It was pure Hawaii inside, and all the doors and windows were thrown open to showcase the view of the beach.

"Oh, it looks fabulous in here," Hollis said. "And it smells fabulous, too."

Sizzling sounds came from the kitchen. Across the restaurant, Sawyer spotted a long table where Kiana, Koa, and their family were seated. It was tucked away from the main area of the restaurant.

"Look at the view," Hollis breathed. The beach did look like paradise.

He led her over to the table. There were hugs and introductions all around. The twins greeted Hollis like a long-lost sister.

"I like your movies, young lady," an older woman said to Hollis.

"Thank you."

Sawyer held a chair out for her. Soon, platters of seafood started arriving.

The conversation and cocktails flowed. Sawyer didn't drink. He wanted to stay alert and protect Hollis, plus he was armed. He wore a holster under his light-weight jacket.

Hollis tried all the dishes.

"These crab cakes are soooo good," she said.

The twins happily told Hollis about all the ingredients and preparation techniques.

Every time she laughed, it made him feel good. He was glad she was having a good time.

His thoughts turned back to that call with her mother. His gut tightened. How could a parent be so... cool and disinterested? He talked with his mom every week. He didn't see her as often as he liked, but he knew she was there for him, the same way he was there for her.

She'd tried to spend more time with him when he first left Ghost Ops—when he was raw and angry. He hadn't always been welcoming, but she never stopped calling.

"I'm so full." Hollis patted her stomach.

"Finish your drink, then I'll show you the deck."

He led her outside, and saw the twins beaming at them. Koa gave him a wink.

The temperature outside had cooled off as the sun was setting. The scent of flowers filled the air. He leaned on the railing, looking at the beach.

"I bet you'll never want to leave here," Hollis said.

"It's become home." He realized it was true. That fact had crept up on him.

"It's helped you heal."

He glanced at her.

"I mean, you haven't said much, but I get the impression what you did in the military wasn't always easy."

"No."

"Will you tell me about it? One day?"

"Maybe." He didn't want her to know the horrible stuff, or his failures.

She nodded, and didn't ask any more questions or make demands.

The bullet took him by surprise.

It whizzed past and hit the glass window right behind Hollis, the crack echoing around them.

Then more gunfire ripped through the evening.

Hollis screamed and Sawyer dived. He took her to the ground and covered her body with his. Glass shattered, raining over them.

Ingrained battle mode washed over Sawyer. His senses became more acute, more focused. *Protect Hollis.* That was all that mattered.

As more shots came, he assessed where the shooter was hiding. The asshole was in some overgrown bushes to the left.

"Stay down," he warned her.

"Sawyer..." Her voice was shaky, terrified.

"It'll be all right. Do not move. Understood?"

"Yes."

He pulled his gun from its holster and rose on one knee. He took aim at the bushes and fired.

The shots stopped, and he heard a grunt.

Sawyer leaped up and over the railing. He fired two more shots in quick succession.

The gunman returned fire and Sawyer dived for cover behind a palm tree. Ducking low, he circled around, moving through the gardens.

The shooting stopped again.

Shit. The shooter had to be making a getaway.

Sawyer abandoned cover, and sprinted, moving in a zigzag pattern. He reached the bushes and found a flattened patch in the vegetation. He looked back and saw that he had a perfect view of the restaurant. There was pandemonium inside.

He searched around, but the asshole was gone.

"*Fuck.*" He sprinted out toward the parking lot.

He caught a glimpse of a man leaping into the back of a car. It sped off, tires screeching.

There was more than one of them. Someone had been driving that getaway car.

He headed back to the restaurant, gun resting at his side.

Hollis was crouched behind an outdoor table. He held out a hand to her.

"He's gone, but I want you inside." He pulled her in through the door, keeping his body between hers and the outside.

As he walked across the restaurant, he pulled out his cellphone and called dispatch. "Shots fired at Mama's restaurant in Paia."

"Shots fired?" The man was Noah, one of their dispatchers.

"Send everyone who's available."

"Sure thing, Sawyer."

He slipped the phone away and looked at Hollis. "You're staying at my place tonight."

HOLLIS WAS numb by the time Sawyer drove her to his cottage. As he parked and turned off the engine, she stared at her hands resting on her lap.

Thankfully, no one had died at the shooting. One woman had been clipped by a bullet and taken to the medical center, but Sawyer had told her that the woman would be fine. Others had been cut by flying glass. The deputies and police had arrived at the restaurant. People had been panicked and scared. The twins had rushed to check that Hollis and Sawyer were okay. She'd been shaky, pumped full of adrenaline.

All she could think about was those bullets whizzing overhead and Sawyer protecting her with his own body.

She'd stayed with the twins while Sawyer had done his deputy thing. She'd liked watching him work, and he was clearly good at it. Around her, people injured by the glass had been treated by the paramedics. She'd tried to help keep some of the injured calm, and had some smears of blood on her dress.

From people who'd been hurt because of her.

This was her fault.

The shooter was after her.

"Hey, come on, you're tired," Sawyer said, jolting her back to the present.

"Someone tried to kill me. *Again*. I just don't understand. I barely heard anything at Reuben's. I don't even understand what I heard—" her voice cracked. "People could've died tonight."

"Hollis—"

She grabbed the skirt of her dress, holding up a stain. "People were bleeding and hurt."

"Hold it together, Hollis. You're strong. *None* of this is your fault. You're the victim here. Hold it together until I can work out who's behind this and stop them." His tone was dark.

God. Sawyer had run after the shooter. What if he'd gotten shot or killed?

Nausea rose in her throat, and she pushed open the SUV door and stumbled out. She sucked in the night air.

"Hollis?"

Strong arms curled around her, and she leaned into him. He made her feel safe. Cared for.

"Let's get inside." He took her hand and tugged her toward the cottage.

It was a standard Hawaiian cottage, painted green with white trim. Neatly trimmed bushes formed the landscaping around the building, and there was a plain, but sturdy, wooden deck. It was simple, but solid and cute.

He led her inside. The inside matched the outside. It was definitely a man's domain, but neat and tidy. She figured it was the military training.

He nudged her onto a leather sofa that was so comfy it swallowed her up. There was a matching armchair, and a huge TV was mounted to the opposite wall. That didn't surprise her. She was pretty sure the Y chromosome required you to need the biggest TV you could find.

"It's time we got more intel." His jaw was tight as he yanked his phone out. Then he cursed.

"What is it?" she asked.

"I've got eleven missed calls from Vander." He put the phone to his ear. "Vander." He paused. "A gunman shot at Hollis in a crowded restaurant tonight. It was a fucking mess." A pause. "She's fine. No one else was hurt badly, just minor injuries." Sawyer pressed a hand to the back of his neck. "What?"

The sharp tone made Hollis jerk. *What now?*

"Okay." He sat beside her and put the phone on the coffee table.

Her belly tied itself in knots.

"It's on speaker," he said.

"Hollis, I'm Vander Norcross," a deep, authoritative voice said.

He sounded like a man who was used to having his orders followed. She cleared her throat. "Hi. I've heard of you. Your company has a good reputation."

"I'm sorry to be talking under these circumstances."

"I'm sorry these circumstances even exist."

Sawyer took her hand and squeezed.

"So, Sawyer told you that we're looking into Michael Reuben."

Her belly flip-flopped. "Yes. Thanks for helping."

"It gets worse. Sawyer, it was why I was trying to call you. But I was too late."

Sawyer tensed. "Go on."

"Someone's put a hit out on Hollis."

Sawyer cursed.

A hit? She blinked. The words didn't make sense, almost as if they were a foreign language.

"Reuben," Sawyer said.

"In all likelihood. We're trying to link him to it." Vander blew out a breath. "The print you sent me...I spoke with a contact at Interpol. It belongs to a contract killer by the name of Gallant. He's experienced, semi-retired, and just takes a few lucrative jobs. He's also meticulous."

"The shooting tonight was *not* meticulous," Sawyer growled. "I've heard of Gallant. He had quite the reputation in his day."

"The shooting doesn't sound like him. He prefers up-close and quiet."

"Like the attack on the beach," Sawyer said grimly.

"Yes. It's said he likes to take souvenirs."

"Oh my God," Hollis breathed. "My favorite bracelet went missing, and a bottle of my perfume."

"That's more Gallant's style," Vander said.

"He was in my house?" She curled her legs up to her chest.

Anger tightened Sawyer's face, and he looked like he wanted to hit someone.

"But the shooting, it isn't his style," Vander continued. "Could be that someone else is also after a paycheck."

"Some tourists posted photos of Hollis online," Sawyer said. "It's public knowledge that she's here."

"Shit." Vander was quiet for a second. "We'll keep digging. Meanwhile, you keep your head down."

Sawyer scraped a hand through his hair. "Vander, I think it's time to send backup."

"I'm already a step ahead of you. Park got out three months ago."

"He did?"

She assumed Park was another Ghost Ops buddy of Sawyer's.

"I never thought he'd leave," Sawyer murmured. "He's almost as good as you with those creepy, on-point instincts."

"He got injured. He bought an isolated cabin in Alaska."

Sawyer frowned. "Hell. Is he okay?"

"Physically, yes. The rest of it, not yet, but he will be."

"I'm not sure sitting alone in the Alaskan wilderness brooding will help."

"I know, that's why I'm sending him to help you in Hawaii."

Sawyer nodded. "Okay. Good."

"Keep it tight, Sawyer. Whoever is after Hollis, you're better than all of them. Hollis, you can trust Sawyer to keep you safe."

"Thanks," she whispered.

"If I get anything else, I'll call."

"Thanks, Vander." Sawyer leaned forward and ended the call.

"I should leave Hawaii," she said.

"What?" His brow creased.

"I put people in danger tonight." She rose and threw her arms in the air. "I need to hide somewhere else."

Where could she go? Tahiti? The Colombian jungle? An Italian monastery?

"You're *not* going anywhere," he growled as he gripped her shoulders. "I told you, I need to know where you are to protect you."

She lifted her chin. "And what if you get hurt?"

"Better than you getting hurt."

"No, it's not. Not to me."

"It's not going to happen." He yanked her against him and kissed her.

It turned hot, desperate, both of them straining against each other. His hand moved across her face, and she felt a lance of pain. She winced.

He pulled back. "What's wrong?" He frowned. "Hell, there's blood on your shoulder. It isn't transfer. *Shit.* There's glass in your neck."

"Really?" She lifted a hand, but he caught her wrist. "I didn't even feel it."

"Probably the adrenaline. You'll feel it soon. We need to clean this."

CHAPTER TWELVE

Hollis was hurt.

Sawyer hated seeing the blood on her dress and skin.

He pulled out his first aid kit from a cupboard in the kitchen. "Dress off."

She shifted with a wince, then pushed the top of her dress down. The entire dress slithered off her, leaving her in a black bra and panties made of gossamer lace.

Sawyer's body locked. Damn, she was beautiful. And hurt. Shoving his desire aside, he made himself focus on the blood on her neck.

There was a small piece of glass embedded in the joint between her neck and shoulder.

She gritted her teeth. "I can feel it now."

"Sit down." He pulled out some tweezers, then sat on the couch beside her. "Hold still." Carefully, he gripped the glass and pulled it out.

"Sawyer, I can't just hide out here, waiting for a

hitman to take a shot at me. If Reuben is behind this, I want to help stop him. I've never played the damsel in distress, and I don't plan to start now."

He set the piece of glass on the table, then pulled out an antiseptic wipe. He gently cleaned her wound.

"Okay, I'll have Vander send us the info that he and his team has. We can do our own digging. Tomorrow, I want you to pack some things from your place."

"We'll stay here?" She looked around. "I like your cottage."

"No, whoever was shooting at Mama's saw me. We'll have to find somewhere else. Somewhere safe."

She sighed. "I bet you wish I'd picked another place to stay. Someone else's coffee machine to set on fire."

He carefully pressed a bandage over her wound, then dropped a kiss to her shoulder. "No, I don't. I'm glad you came to my island, Hollis Stanton."

Her fingers curled around his jaw and her mouth touched his. She leaned into him, moaning as she deepened the kiss.

"No." He pulled back reluctantly.

She groaned. "Is this that, 'I'm vulnerable and need to rest' thing again?"

"Yes. I want to take care of you, protect you."

"Be careful, Sawyer. I could fall for you." She rose. "I'm going to borrow a toothbrush and a T-shirt."

He watched her disappear into his bedroom. Hell, Hollis Stanton was in his bedroom.

I could fall for you.

Shit. He rose and checked the house, locking the

127

doors. He pulled out his phone and checked the exterior cameras he had installed when he first moved in. He adjusted the tolerance on the alerts. If anyone tried to sneak up on them, he'd know.

When he entered his bedroom, he found Hollis wearing his T-shirt, and sitting cross legged on his bed. His cock took a lot of notice. That red hair was loose and looked as soft as silk.

He'd never had a type before, but he did now. *Hollis*.

Damn, he liked seeing her in his T-shirt.

He took a quick shower and pulled on some boxer shorts. He turned the lights off and sat on the edge of the bed. Hollis was already under the sheet, but tossing and turning. She whacked the pillow.

"Hollis, you need to relax."

"That is impossible." She flopped backward on the bed. "The shooting just keeps running through my head." Then she lifted her head. "Are you getting into bed?"

Sawyer rubbed his jaw. "I've...never slept in this bed."

She sat up, watching him carefully. "Never?"

"I've tried." He released a breath. He hated talking about this. "I don't sleep well. I just take a few catnaps. Usually in my armchair."

She was quiet for a moment. "You mentioned this before. And Benny did too. You have trouble getting to sleep?"

"Yeah. And staying asleep." He shrugged. "I'm used to it. I don't need a lot of sleep."

"Everyone needs to rest, Sawyer. I've been having nightmares since this Reuben thing started." She smiled.

"Except when I'm sleeping with you." She cocked her head. "You slept in bed with me at my place the other night."

"I did. Had the best few hours sleep I've had in a long time."

She held out a hand. "Then maybe you just need me beside you."

He took her elegant hand in his, and let her tug him down beside her.

"Besides, I need you or I won't sleep," she said. "I just can't get my brain to turn off. I keep hearing the gunshots, seeing the broken glass everywhere, people screaming..."

"I guess I'll have to help you sleep."

"What—?"

He pulled her over his body until she straddled him.

"Sawyer—"

He dropped back until he was flat on the bed and then yanked her until she straddled his upper chest. She reached out and gripped the headboard.

"What are you doing?" Her voice was breathy. "I thought I was too vulnerable?"

"For other things, but not for me taking care of you. I'm going to eat your pussy, and make you come so hard you'll sleep."

Her face flushed. "Oh."

"On my face, gorgeous."

"I don't—"

He cupped her ass and pulled her forward. As he'd guessed, she wasn't wearing any panties under his T-shirt. His mouth found slick folds.

"*Oh, God.* Oh, oh—"

He licked and sucked. Fuck, he loved the taste of her. Soon, she was making sweet sounds.

"*Sawyer,*" she moaned. Her hips rocked as she rode his face.

"Been dreaming of this for days."

"You have?" She was breathless.

He speared his tongue inside her, then shifted, and licked her swollen clit.

"I'm close, I'm—" Her release broke and her body shuddered. She chanted his name, and it was the best thing he'd ever heard.

When she collapsed, she rolled onto the pillow beside him. Her hair was spread everywhere, her chest rising and falling fast. She looked up at him lazily, with a satisfied smile.

"Relaxed now?" he asked.

"Yes." She reached for him. "Let me touch—"

"No." He pressed her hand back to the bed. "That was for you."

She blinked sleepily. "I really like you."

Shit. Sawyer felt things he hadn't felt in a long time. Or ever. "I really like you, too."

She snuggled into the pillow, losing her battle against sleep. "Don't get hurt, Sawyer. Don't run off. The people I care about never seem to care back as much. They always leave. I think something in me is broken."

"You're not broken, baby." That was on them, not her.

But she was already asleep. He leaned over and pressed a kiss to her cheek. He slipped out of bed and brushed his teeth again. When he lay back down, she made a sound and shifted toward him.

So damn trusting, and he knew she was a woman who didn't trust easily.

He wrapped an arm around her. "Whatever it takes, I'll protect you."

SCREAMS.

Smoke.

Flames.

Horror.

"Sawyer? Please, wake up."

A voice pierced the nightmare.

"Sawyer, you're okay. You're on Maui. You're with me."

He opened his eyes, his body tense and his chest heaving.

"Sawyer?" she asked carefully.

Hollis. "I'm awake."

"You were having a nightmare." She shifted on the bed.

"Don't turn on the lamp," he said quickly.

She paused. "Okay."

He wiped a hand over his face, and let the last vestiges of the bad memories leak away.

Her hand pressed against his chest. Again, she didn't ask any questions, and he closed his eyes.

"I'm sorry," she whispered.

"You have nothing to be sorry about."

"I'm just sorry you have bad memories that haunt you."

He pressed his hand over hers, and something welled up inside him. It was a part of him that he didn't usually share. He sat up and jerked off the bed. "Go back to sleep."

"Sawyer—"

He strode into the darkened living room, his mind and gut churning. His hands squeezed into fists, then relaxed. He crossed to the armchair and dropped heavily into it. He didn't think he'd get back to sleep.

A faint whisper of sound. He smelled Hollis's sweet scent.

"Go back to bed, Hollis. I'm sorry I woke you."

"You're going to sleep out here?"

"Yeah." There was no way he'd sleep.

She was quiet, then she moved. He closed his eyes.

When she lowered herself onto his lap, his eyes popped open.

"Then I'm sleeping here with you." She snuggled into his chest. He slid an arm around her, and she pressed a quick kiss to his pec. "This is pretty comfy."

Sawyer buried his face in her hair and held on. For once, the darkness didn't seem so thick, or the shadows so menacing. They sat like that for a while, her body warm against his.

"I was on a mission." The words spilled out of him.

She tensed for a second, then relaxed. He felt her fingers brush up and down his forearm. A small, grounding touch.

"I'd been training some Afghan soldiers." God, it hurt

to talk about it. "They were the best of the best. We were doing really advanced stuff, and I became good friends with one of the men. Tabish." Sawyer couldn't help but smile. Tabish had been the owner of a hell of a laugh. "He wanted a better future for his country, for his family, and for his daughters. He had two little girls." Sawyer let out a shuddering breath.

Hollis pressed into him.

"There were plenty of people who didn't want us training the troops."

"The Taliban," she murmured.

"Yes. One day, Tabish didn't show up at training. I was told he'd left the base. It wasn't like him. I found out that he'd gotten word that there was going to be an attack on his village. I went after him."

Hollis pressed a hand to his stomach. "Take a breath."

He realized his chest was heaving quickly. He obeyed, and took a deep breath. "When I got there, his village was on fire. The Taliban were punishing Tabish... and me. I'd had a skirmish with a local warlord a few weeks prior. I'd cost him a lot of money when he didn't get his poppy harvests."

"What happened?"

"Tabish had been beaten and tied up. They had him on his knees in front of his burning house. The warlord's men had locked people in their homes. Including Tabish's family."

"Oh, God," she breathed.

Pain seared through Sawyer.

"When I arrived, I took out as many of the fighters as

I could." He'd taken a bullet. "The rest of them left. They'd achieved what they'd come for."

Screams and smoke.

"I'm sorry, Sawyer. Sorry that the world has such horrible people in it. It wasn't your fault."

"I know that, but I feel like it was anyway."

She held him tighter. "What happened to Tabish?"

"When I untied him, he walked into the flames of his house."

"Sawyer..."

He held her and pulled her close, a hand tangling in her hair. "I like to think they're all in a better place. That they're together." His hand tightened. "You can't get hurt, Hollis. You can't die."

"I'm right here. It's okay. Just hold me."

He did, but it was a long time before they both fell asleep again.

"MY WORLD-FAMOUS BREAKFAST WRAP." Hollis carried the plates out onto the deck.

It was a bright, sunny day. Maui was doing its best to chase off the last of any nightmares and assassination attempts.

Sawyer sat in a wooden chair, cradling his coffee mug.

"Another world-famous Hollis Stanton breakfast." He shot her a small smile. "Thanks."

She could tell the night was still weighing on him,

hence her efforts to cheer him up with food. And to take her mind off her own troubles.

"You sure it's okay to sit out here." She glanced around nervously, half expecting a shooter to pop up.

He reached out and touched her arm. "Jesse and another deputy are patrolling around here until we leave. I've already checked in with them."

She nodded

She set her feet on the railing. Beyond, the ocean glinted in the distance. "Hey, is that the roof of my place? Archer's place?"

"Yes."

She bit into her egg wrap. *Yum*. The taste of eggs and melted cheese hit her tastebuds.

"I thought actresses only ate salad," Sawyer said, with a wry smile.

She took another generous bite. "And we have three assistants, and an entourage, and we carry tiny, fluffy dogs in our purses."

He grinned. "Yeah."

"And I thought former soldiers only wore camo gear, and had so many guns there was nowhere to put them, and spent their weekends prepping for the apocalypse."

That got her a bigger, more natural smile. "Touché."

She liked that smile. After what he'd shared with her, he deserved some happiness. She was touched that he'd shared some of his past. Her heart had broken for him, and his lost friend.

"I do work out more, and watch my food more when I'm prepping for a big role," she told him. "Otherwise, I just try to stay active and eat pretty healthy. Thankfully, I also have a fast metabolism."

"I'm glad you don't eat just salad." He ate some of his own wrap, then he paused for a moment. "Vander sent through everything his tech guy, Ace, assembled on Michael Reuben."

Reality felt like a big drop of sludge hitting the back of her neck. "All right."

"And Leilani is organizing some secure laptops and VPNs for us. But before we do more research, we need to move."

"Move?"

"I told you that Archer's place and my place aren't safe."

Her stomach twisted. "Your life's been so disrupted—"

"Enough with that." He grabbed her hand. "I'm glad I'm here keeping you safe."

She was, too.

"We'll have to leave our phones behind, in case the men hunting you have the capabilities to trace them and listen to your calls."

Oh, God. She swallowed. Suddenly, breakfast was just a bad taste in her mouth.

"I have a burner phone we can use," he continued.

Suddenly, Hollis's cellphone rang, making her jolt. "It's Tavion."

"Tell him he won't be able to get in touch with you for a bit."

She nodded and answered the call. "Hi, Tave."

"Fuck, Hollis, are you all right?" He sounded frantic.

"Yes, I—"

"It's all over the Internet," Tave said. "A shooting at a restaurant on Maui. There was a picture of you in the middle of the shot-up restaurant. Were you injured?"

"I'm okay. I'm not hurt."

"Lane said he'd take care of you, but this is *not* what I had in mind."

"He saved my life, Tave. Again. The shooter was after me. Someone's put a hit out on me."

The line went silent. "What the fuck?" His voice vibrated with rage. "I'm going to find Reuben and rip his balls off."

"Tavion, I'm okay. Look, Sawyer said I need to ditch my phone. He's going to take me somewhere safe."

Her agent cursed. "I hate the idea of having no contact, but if it keeps you safe... Hols, I did some digging on Lane. He has the skills to keep you breathing."

"I know." She met Sawyer's gaze. "And I trust him."

"All right, Red. You take care of yourself, and as soon as you can, you call me."

"I will, Tave."

She ended the call and handed the phone to Sawyer. He powered it down. Then Sawyer's cellphone rang.

He pressed it to his ear. "Lane. Hi, Koa. What did you find?" A pause. "That's perfect. I owe you. And remember, you can't mention this to anyone." Another pause, then an eyeroll. "Yes, I'll get her autograph for your uncle."

He slipped the phone away. "I put out feelers for somewhere we can stay."

"And you found something?"

"Koa came through. His uncle's best friend's cousin has a cottage in Upcountry."

"Upcountry?"

"It's the area in central Maui, on the slopes of Mount Haleakala. We can stay there until I find this hitman, and arrest him."

Worry nipped at her.

"It's going to be okay." He kissed her fingers. "I promise."

CHAPTER THIRTEEN

Sawyer's hands gripped the wheel of the truck he'd borrowed from Benny. It was old, but his cousin kept the Toyota Tacoma running smoothly.

They made their way up the winding, scenic road. Here, Maui was all rolling hills and lush volcanic soil, where the locals farmed taro and sweet potatoes.

Hollis had been quiet for most of the drive. He reached over and gave her leg a squeeze.

"You okay?"

She turned her head. "Sort of." She sent him a small smile. "Don't worry, I'll shake it off. I'm just having a little pity party."

"We're going to sort this out, Hollis. I won't let you get hurt."

She covered his hand with hers. "I'm glad you're with me."

Before long, they drove into the area of Kula. "The cottage isn't far from here," he told her.

"We're close to the volcano?"

"Yes, on the western slopes of Haleakala. It's a massive shield volcano that forms seventy-five percent of the island." He smiled. "Don't worry, it hasn't erupted for over five hundred years."

She pulled a face. "My luck hasn't been that great lately, so don't jinx it."

"You know, this area is also known for its flowers. It's where most of the cut flowers used in leis come from."

"It is beautiful up here."

They drove for a few more minutes. Sawyer spotted the mailbox, and turned onto a gravel driveway.

"Oh, wow." She leaned forward. "And I thought Archer's place had a great view."

The cottage was perched on the side of the hill. The sweeping views were stunning. Mountains and lush, rolling hills lay before them, and there was a clear view all the way to the ocean.

They climbed out and Sawyer got their bags out of the back. Hollis carried the small bag of food they'd brought from his place. He'd scavenged what he could from his fridge and pantry. It would keep them going for a bit.

He found the key under the potted plant by the door, and unlocked it. The place was simple, with a wood floor and sturdy furniture. It was more like his place than Archer's.

He set the bags in the bedroom. There was a double bed with a simple, white cover on it.

"The place isn't fancy," he warned her.

She stood at the wooden kitchen island, looking out the glass doors past the deck to the hills beyond. She stiffened. "I don't need fancy. Are you waiting for me to go diva on you? Demand Italian mineral water, or pull that fluffy dog out of my handbag?"

He rested his hands on her shoulders. "No. I know you're not like that."

She huffed. "Sorry, I'm acting like a bitch. I'm just—"

"Stressed and worried."

"Right."

He kissed her. "I'm here. Whatever you need."

"I know. Thank you, Sawyer. I'm going to freshen up, then—" her tone sharpened "—I'm going to dig into Michael Reuben's life. I'm *not* going to sit around waiting for his hired assassin to kill me."

He loved that courage. "We might make a SEAL out of you yet."

"Hardly. I don't sleep on the ground, or go camping. I need a real bed and a bathroom. Maybe there is a little diva in me after all." She disappeared into the bathroom.

Sawyer pulled out one of the laptops. He also needed to do a security sweep of the cottage and set up some cameras he'd brought with him. No one was sneaking up on them.

In the kitchen, he pulled out his bag of coffee and put on the coffee machine. Hollis could have a caffeine hit. He was relieved that they were where no one could find them. Her safety was important to him. He opened some cupboards, and pulled out a mug. Her happiness was also important to him.

She was important to him.

Shit. He stilled. He'd steered clear of letting

people get too close for a long time. Watching the people you cared for get hurt or die... It cut too deep.

Damn. He hadn't even realized how much he'd cut himself off after he'd left Ghost Ops. He'd come to an island in the middle of the ocean. He couldn't cut himself off more than that.

Luckily, Benny and his family had been a lifeline.

Then Hollis had blasted through his defenses. Without even trying.

Sawyer shook his head. He couldn't think of that, or his feelings for her, right now. His first priority was getting her safe.

"Oh, coffee. My hero." She moved up beside him and pressed a kiss to his arm. Then she reached out and poured. "You want one?"

He shook his head. "I'm going outside to do a security sweep."

She gave him a salute. "Yes, sir."

"That's a pretty good salute."

"I had to learn how to do it properly for a movie. It was a bit part that got cut in the editing phase." She touched his arm. "Be careful out there."

He nodded. "I won't be long."

Hollis sat at the table in front of the open laptop.

"Use the VPN. We don't want anyone tracking us here."

She nodded. "Let's see what I can dig up." She cracked her knuckles. "If I can manage not to get distracted by that view." She nodded at the picture window.

Sawyer left her to it and stepped outside. Instantly, he missed her. He hated having her out of his sight.

She'll leave you one day.

His chest squeezed painfully. Her life was in LA, and his was here. He wouldn't do well in the city, and he sure as hell didn't belong at the glitzy parties and red-carpet premieres of a movie star.

You're getting ahead of yourself, Lane.

He wandered around the cottage and set up his cameras. They'd alert him to any movement.

Back inside, Hollis was bent over the laptop, her brow furrowed. She didn't even hear him approach.

"How's it going?"

She jumped. "You scared me."

"Sorry, but you should have more situational awareness."

She waved a hand at him. "I'm going over Vander's intel on Reuben. The guy's so shady. Why do so many people work with him?"

"Money and power. It hides the worst of it."

"Why are some people so horrible?" she murmured.

Those old memories bit at him. "I have no answer for that. But I do know there are good people out there too."

Her lips quirked. "Over a decade in the movie business made me lose hope." Her gaze locked with his. "You made me believe again."

HOLLIS RUBBED HER ACHING EYES. She'd been staring at the screen for way too long. Her computer skills were a little rusty. To be honest, she didn't spend a lot of time on a computer.

The remnants of dinner sat at the end of the table. Sawyer had brought some fish with them in a cooler bag, and cooked it with a coconut sauce. It had been really good.

She looked over at him. He was on a second laptop, and the glow of the screen made shadows on the dips and hollows of his rugged face.

She got a funny sensation in her stomach. She had feelings for him. She'd never felt so close to someone so quickly before. She tucked a strand of hair behind her ear as a tickle of nerves skittered through her. She'd only known the man a week, but it felt like far longer.

There was no way he'd like life in LA. She couldn't imagine him there. She remembered that nightmare he'd had. He'd suffocate in LA. Hell, she liked the city, and sometimes she felt like she was suffocating.

She knew she was setting herself up for heartache.

One day, he'd be gone, and she'd be all alone. Again.

How about you focus on staying alive first, Hols?

"Did you see the photos Vander sent?"

Sawyer's voice made her jolt.

"No." She opened the email. "Photos of what?"

She'd been focused on Reuben. Vander's team had dug up tons of details, and now she knew more about Reuben's life than she'd ever wanted to.

"Not what, who," Sawyer said. "Of possible hitmen that took the contract."

Her belly shriveled to a sharp point. It was still hard to believe Reuben had hired someone to kill her.

Photos appeared on the computer screen. They were all of hard-eyed men, and one woman.

What kind of person killed for money? She clicked through them.

Then a face filled the screen. The man was older, with a long face and a cleft in his chin. His dark hair was threaded with gray. She froze, and just stared.

"Hollis?" The scrape of a chair. Sawyer's hands rested on her shoulders and squeezed. "You recognize him?"

"Not exactly. I...never got a clear look at the man on the beach. The sun was wrong, and he was shadowed and wearing a mask. But I think I saw this man in Paia. Coming out of a shop wearing a horrible Hawaiian shirt."

Sawyer cursed. "That's Joseph Gallant and he's bad news."

"The hitman that Vander mentioned. The one who takes souvenirs." She hated the idea that this man had been creeping around her house, taking her things.

"He's dangerous because he's good, and quick, and efficient. I think he's the man who attacked you on the beach, but keep looking at the photos. I'm thinking there is more than one asshole hunting you. There were definitely at least two people at Mama's."

"More than one person out to kill me? You've got to be joking." She shoved her chair back. She couldn't stay sitting there any longer.

"Hollis—"

"I need... I have no idea what I need." She took a few steps, her heart beating hard. "I want to punch Michael Reuben in the face. Why does he think he can end my life?" She shook her head. "I'm sick of being anxious and afraid. Worried that someone will attack me." Or hurt Sawyer. Somehow, she'd gotten very lucky when this man had arrived to turn off her smoke alarm.

"Gorgeous." He spun her to face him. Then he cupped her jaw and kissed her.

The kiss was slow, and oh, so sexy. With a low moan, she leaned into him. His strong arms closed around her.

"That," she murmured. "That's what I needed."

"You're not alone in this. I'm right here."

She hugged him hard. His big hand pressed against her back. A part of her was so afraid to lean on him, to get used to him being there, and that one day she'd wake up, and he'd be gone.

She lifted her head. "Reuben needs to be stopped. Whatever he's into can't be good. And the fact that he hired someone to kill me—" she shook her head "—or more than one person... I'm going to take him down."

Sawyer smiled. "Hell, yeah. We'll take him down together."

CHAPTER FOURTEEN

H ollis woke and stared blindly at the unfamiliar bedroom. Sunshine was shining in through the thin curtains.

Everything rushed back in. They were in Upcountry. Assassins were hunting her.

But Sawyer was with her.

She turned her head and looked at him beside her. Her heart did a hard thump. He was still asleep. Propping her head up on her hand, she took her time looking at that rugged face. His big body made the bed feel tiny.

His eyes opened.

"Morning," she murmured. "I like watching you sleep. In a very uncreepy way."

He focused on her. "What time is it?"

She glanced at the clock on the nightstand. "A little after six-thirty."

"Really?" He sat up and swung his feet off the bed. He bent over, his elbows resting on his knees.

She stared at his back and frowned. "Sawyer?" She crawled across the bed. "What's wr—?"

Suddenly, he grabbed her and hauled her onto his lap. She gasped and grabbed his arms.

"I slept through the night." His voice was a little hoarse. "I slept through the night, with no nightmares, and your body tucked up beside me."

Her heartbeat echoed in her ears. "Yes."

He pressed his forehead to hers. "Haven't slept through the night for two years, Hollis."

Emotions swelled inside her.

"You're a fucking miracle," he whispered.

"No." She gripped the sides of his face. "We're just good together."

He smiled. "We are."

"And now, I'm going to make us breakfast. Or try to, since we don't have much food."

His brow creased. "I'll need to go into Kula and get supplies. Too dangerous to take you with me, but I don't like leaving you alone."

"It'll be fine. Let's worry about that after we eat and shower."

"We showering together?"

She smiled. "Yes. One, it saves water. Two, I want to see you naked." She slid off him and stood. "And three, I'm planning to suck your cock while we're in there."

His big body locked. Oh, it gave her a hit of pleasure to see him react like that.

"You onboard with my plan, Deputy Lane?" she asked saucily.

He gave her a long, hot look. "Yeah, Ms. Stanton, I am."

After a quick breakfast, and a long, pleasurable shower, Hollis found herself in the compact living area, watching Sawyer getting ready to head into town. They'd wiped out most of the food they'd brought with them from Sawyer's at breakfast.

"I won't be gone long."

"I'll be fine." She wasn't sure if she was reassuring him or herself.

"You could come, but I don't want anyone to see you." He lifted his head, a serious look on his face. "You'd need to stay in the truck. There's always a chance someone would spot you. They'll be looking for a redhead—"

"I'll be fine here," she repeated again.

"Don't answer the door."

"Yes, Dad."

He hauled her close. "Believe me, I have no fatherly feelings toward you, especially after our shower." He took her mouth in a quick kiss.

Just that small touch left her lightheaded.

"Here." He held something out to her.

She stared at the handgun. "No." She held up her hands. "I don't like guns."

"Take it, Hollis. Until I get back. Can you use it?"

She sighed and took it. "Yes. I had to train with handguns for a movie once."

He nodded. "I'll be back as soon as I can."

"Okay."

She watched him leave. She stayed in the doorway

until the truck disappeared from view. *Ugh*. Stress immediately tightened her neck and shoulders. She decided she needed to do something.

Bake. She'd bake something. She hardly ever got the chance.

Opening the pantry, she studied the contents. Luckily, the cottage was equipped with all the basics like sugar, flour, and long-life milk. She got the ingredients out, set the oven to heat up, then started mixing. The kitchen wasn't fancy, and the cabinetry and counters were old, but it was meticulously clean.

As she mixed, she turned to look at the view. She couldn't decide if she preferred the rolling hills or the ocean. They were both stunning.

She glanced at the gun sitting on the countertop and shuddered. Setting the bowl down, she wiped her hands on a kitchen towel, then grabbed the gun. She crossed to a wooden cabinet and set the gun on top.

It made her feel better that it was out of sight.

Back in the kitchen, she opened some drawers looking for a baking tray. Ah hah. She pulled out a frypan to get to the tray. After greasing it, she put the cookies on the tray, and slid them into the oven.

Right, what next? Her gaze fell on the laptop at the dining table. Time to get back to work.

Hollis tucked her legs beneath her on the chair and got searching. She continued digging deeper into Reuben's life. Instead of focusing on his recent history, she was looking into his earlier life. There was a short gap in his early schooling. He'd been born and raised in California, but there wasn't any record of his first few years of school. It was weird.

Maybe he'd been homeschooled? She wasn't sure, but something felt off. She'd keep looking into it.

The oven dinged. Rising, she pulled the cookies out and set them on the counter to cool.

She looked out the window, her gaze drawn to an orange-and-black butterfly fluttering around one of the bushes. Oh, she guessed it was a Kamehameha butterfly. The state insect of Hawaii.

More movement.

That's when she caught a glimpse of a man disappearing into the bushes near the cottage.

Her blood ran cold.

No. Someone had found them.

She stood there frozen and got another glimpse of him. He was heading toward the house.

Hollis came to life and raced over to the front door and checked that it was locked. Then, she quickly moved down the short hall to the back door, and made sure that was locked, too.

Were those footfalls she could hear on the deck outside? Fear was hot in her veins as she raced back to the kitchen.

What to do? Should she hide?

As she was churning over her choices, she heard a noise.

In the *hallway*.

Oh, God. He was inside.

She dropped down behind the island. She peered around the edge and saw the man emerge from the hall.

Her heart leaped into her throat. *How did he get in?*

He was tall and solid, with black hair shaved very short. He'd probably be considered handsome, if not for the flat look in his eyes, the scar on his jaw, and the intense vibe he gave off.

This man was a killer.

God, the gun was across the room. She squeezed her eyes closed. It was too far away.

She stayed crouched in the kitchen, trying to stay calm. He hadn't spotted her. Yet.

Her throat was tight, and her breathing fast. She needed a weapon. She'd hit the guy, then escape. She'd hide until Sawyer got back.

She dragged in a deep breath, pushing her fear down. She could do this.

Her gaze snagged on the handle of the frying pan that she'd left on the counter earlier. Slowly, she reached up and grabbed the handle. Carefully and slowly, she slid the pan toward her and off the counter. She clutched it to her chest. It was made of iron and very sturdy.

Her grip tightened on the handle. She didn't hear the man, but she sensed him getting closer.

You can do this, Hollis.

She leaped up and rounded the counter. She swung the frying pan.

The man cursed and dodged. It hit his shoulder with a solid whack.

Hollis threw herself at him, trying to hit him again. He knocked the frying pan out of her hand. It hit the floor with a loud clatter. She stumbled into him and threw him off balance. He went down on the floor, and she leaped over him.

Get out. That was the only thought in her head.

A hand snapped out and gripped her ankle. She fell. She hit the floor hard, winding herself. *Ow, ow, ow.* She tried to kick him.

"Dammit, wait." His voice was harsh.

She glanced at him, her gaze landing on the scars on his jaw and neck. And cold, dark eyes.

Fear pumped through her, and she tried to break free. She kicked and flailed like crazy.

He launched at her, and landed on top of her. She heaved her body up, and they rolled.

"Listen—"

Hell, no. She wasn't listening to anything this man had to say. She'd fight and she'd survive.

God, she wanted Sawyer.

They rolled again and bumped into the coffee table.

Hollis reached up, slapping her hand on the surface of the table. Her fingers closed on the glass bowl resting on it. She yanked it off and threw it at him.

But the angle was awkward, and it barely brushed him.

He cursed, and she tried to get to her feet. He grabbed a handful of her shirt and yanked her down.

Dammit. Her heart was thundering, and she could barely think.

"Just hold still and—"

"*No.*" She rammed an elbow into his jaw. With a growl, he rolled on top of her and pinned her down.

No.

The door burst open.

Relief flooded her.

Sawyer came in—face set like stone—his gun aimed at her attacker.

AS SAWYER HEADED up to the cottage, he tensed. He heard a struggle inside.

Hollis was fighting with someone.

He dropped the grocery bags and yanked his weapon from its holster. He raced up the steps and kicked the door in.

Instantly, he saw Hollis on the floor, pinned under a man's strong body.

He lifted the gun and aimed it at the man's head.

Then Sawyer froze, lowered the weapon, and smiled. "Park?"

"Sawyer." The lean, dangerous man lifted his chin. He'd always had an edge, but now it had been honed sharp. His face was leaner, his gaze darker.

A man with demons.

"Wait?" Hollis said. "You know him?"

"I do." Sawyer crossed the room and held out a hand. "Do you mind getting off my woman?"

Park slapped a hand into Sawyer's, and Sawyer hauled him to his feet. Then Sawyer helped Hollis up off the floor, keeping her close.

"Damn good to see you," Sawyer said.

Park's lips lifted. "You too."

Then they were hugging and slapping each other's backs.

"I'm guessing this means he's not one of the hitmen?" Hollis asked.

"No. Hollis Stanton, meet Parker Conroy. A buddy of mine."

She blinked. "Um, hi."

Park nodded.

"Vander sent him to help me keep you safe."

"Oh, well—" she pulled a face "—sorry for swinging a frying pan at you."

Sawyer raised his brows.

"What about the glass bowl?" Park nodded at the bowl upside down on the floor.

"That barely hit you," she said. "I thought you were an assassin here to kill me."

Park's lips moved, and Sawyer knew that was the closest thing they'd get to a smile.

"I'd better rescue the groceries," Sawyer said. "And fix the front door."

"Bring the groceries in and I'll make some lunch for all of us," Hollis said.

Soon, Hollis was busy in the kitchen. After Park and Sawyer used tools from the truck to fix the door, they headed out on the deck. They both held mugs of coffee and freshly-made cookies.

"Hell, that's a view." Park looked at the sweep of hillside.

Sawyer sipped. "Vander bring you up to speed?"

"Yeah. He had a dossier for me to read on Reuben on

the private jet over here. Sounds like a nasty piece of work." Park bit into a cookie.

Sawyer nodded. "Not all the bad guys are warlords. Some are harder to spot."

"I prefer the warlords."

"But you got out. I never thought you would." If there was ever a man born for the job of Ghost Ops, it was Parker Conroy.

Park looked at the view again. "I...just couldn't anymore." He rubbed the scars on his neck.

"You okay?"

"I healed up fine. The doctors put me back together. There was an explosion, and the recovery sucked."

"I don't just mean the physical recovery."

The man's fingers tightened on his coffee mug. "I'm fit for duty. I'll help you protect her."

"I don't doubt that." Sawyer paused. "I get it, Park. I was there not long ago."

"I'll be fine." His tone was clipped.

Sawyer nodded. He'd leave it. For now.

"So, you hooked up with Hollywood's hottest actress?"

"It's—" Sawyer wanted to say more than a hook up, but was it? Hollis would eventually go back to LA and leave him behind. "She's smart, beautiful... And I'm not letting her get hurt."

Park sipped his coffee. "You've got my help, but man, you need to admit to yourself that you're in love with her."

Sawyer's heart skipped a beat. "No. I've only known her a week."

Park lifted a dark brow.

"What the hell do you know about love anyway?" Sawyer said.

"Not a thing, but I have eyes. I can see just fine."

Sawyer shook his head. "That's not what's important right now. There are hitmen on this island who want her dead. That's *not* going to happen."

Park gave him the faintest smile. "Luckily, Hollis has two Ghost Ops soldiers at her back. And she has a pretty mean swing with a frying pan."

If the hitmen tried again, they wouldn't know what hit them.

"I'm glad you're here, man."

Park lifted his mug, chinking it against Sawyer's. "Happy to be here."

CHAPTER FIFTEEN

Hollis listened to the low rumble of Sawyer and Parker talking. She glanced out at them on the deck. It was clear that they were good friends.

She chewed her lip. She didn't have close friends like that. She had Tavion, and she trusted him, but they didn't hang out a lot because they were both so busy. He was as much of a workaholic as she was. She had plenty of acquaintances, some who would stab her in the back to get a role if they needed to.

Everything in her life was about work. The next movie, the next premiere, the next potential Oscar win.

Life had been whizzing past, and she hadn't stopped to smell the roses. Hell, she hadn't even stopped to smell a daisy.

This entire situation with Reuben had brought her life sharply into focus.

She looked back at the laptop screen and made herself concentrate. It wasn't the time to have an almost-midlife crisis while she was being hunted by a hitman. Or hitmen.

Information popped up on the screen and she leaned forward. Her pulse spiked.

It couldn't be.

She checked the photo again.

"Sawyer," she called out.

He walked in from the deck, and looking at him distracted her for a second. She just loved the way he walked, so in control of that big, powerful body.

"What have you got?"

Parker entered silently, standing nearby like a dark shadow.

"There was this weird gap in Reuben's early schooling record. He only started school in the fourth grade. So I did a bit more digging."

"He went to another school?"

"If he did, I can't find a record of it. But I did some searches of children's groups in the town where he was born—sports teams, choirs, dance groups. Anything I could think of. I found a reference to a boy his age in a choir." She tapped and a picture appeared with a bunch of smiling kids standing in two rows. She zoomed in on a dark-haired, dark-eyed boy with a long nose. He wasn't smiling.

"Reuben," Sawyer said.

"It doesn't give a surname, but he's listed as Mikhail in this picture."

"Russian," Sawyer breathed. "He's Russian."

Hollis tapped on the keyboard. "His parents names were Alex and Natalie Reuben."

Sawyer frowned.

Excitement whipped through her as she kept tapping. "Strange thing is, there is no record of Alex and Natalie Reuben's parents. There are names listed, but no history comes up for them. No addresses, no social security numbers."

"Shit," Park muttered.

"His parents were probably Russian sleeper agents," Sawyer said. "Reuben was born here, but his parents weren't. His allegiance is to Russia."

Hollis gasped. "Sleeper agents? Really? That isn't just something in spy movies?"

"No," Sawyer replied.

"He's moving shipments of something to or from Russia," Park said. "Something important."

Sawyer nodded and his brow creased. Then his cellphone dinged. "Vander wants a video call."

Hollis reached out and tapped on the laptop screen. A second later, the call connected, and the face of a handsome, dark-haired man appeared. Even across the computer screen, an intensity radiated off him that made Parker seem chill.

"Hollis," the man said.

"Vander," she replied. "It's nice to officially meet you."

"One day, I hope it's in person and under different circumstances."

"Vander." Sawyer leaned forward over her shoulder. "Hollis has been digging into Reuben's background. He's Russian. His name was Mikhail. We suspect he's the son of sleeper agents."

"That makes sense. We discovered what his shipments are." Vander's face sharpened. "Weapons. He's smuggling high-tech, classified weapons back to Russia via the Port of Los Angeles. Hidden on cargo vessels."

Sawyer cursed.

A muscle ticked in Vander's jaw. "Some of it is experimental, military grade stuff. Drones, missiles, AI weapons technology."

"He's got to be stopped," Sawyer clipped out.

"Oh, he will be. I've made some calls to friends of the federal kind. They're working on arrest warrants now."

"Warrants." Hollis felt her chest hitch. "He's going to go to jail? I'll be safe?"

Vander's dark gaze narrowed. "Eventually. The problem is the contract he's put out on your life is still active. A lot of contract killers refuse to stop a job once they're on it. To keep their reputation intact."

Oh, God. It felt like this was never going to end. Sawyer's hands landed on her shoulders.

"Ace has been combing security footage at Maui airport. He clocked these three."

Pictures of three men flashed up on the screen.

They all looked like non-descript white men. One had a beard, one had a shaved head, and the other had dirty blonde hair.

"They're a kill team," Vander said. "They're ex-Serbian military, and they work together. The one with the beard is the leader. Ivan Stankovic." Vander's gaze flicked to Sawyer. "And they're known for making a mess. They don't believe in subtle or stealthy."

"Cowboys." Park's voice was filled with disdain.

"They're likely the ones who shot up Mama's," Sawyer said.

Hollis pressed her fingers to her eyes. "So, I have an ice cold, experienced assassin after me, along with three crazy people who want me dead."

"No one is dying here," Sawyer growled.

"Ace is trying to track them," Vander said. "I'm glad Parker is there now too, as these three might be cowboys, but they are good at tracking down their targets."

Ice filled her veins.

"All of you, lay low and stay out of sight. We'll find these guys, and you can eliminate them."

Hollis swallowed. "Eliminate?"

Vander's lips twitched. "That means we'll have Sawyer's sheriff friends arrest them."

She released a breath. "Oh, right."

Sawyer squeezed her shoulders. "Thanks, Vander."

He nodded. "Hang in there. This will be all over soon."

Hollis sure hoped so.

SAWYER WAS SLOWLY MOVING inside Hollis.

They were locked in the bedroom, with Parker sleeping on the couch. They had to be quiet. Sawyer didn't want his buddy hearing them.

She looked up at him, and God, the look on her face made his gut lock.

"Gorgeous," he murmured. "So gorgeous."

"*Sawyer.*"

He hiked one of her legs higher, and felt her muscles clenching his cock. Damn, he wouldn't last much longer.

Here. Right here was what he'd been searching for since he'd left the military. A sense of home, belonging, acceptance.

He picked up the pace of his thrusts, and Hollis got noisier. Her low moans filled the room. He pressed a palm over her mouth. "Quiet, baby."

Her eyes flashed, and he could tell she liked it. Her tongue licked his palm, and she arched up into him.

On his next thrust, she started coming. Her teeth bit into his palm. He couldn't hold back. Her release triggered his and he bit down on his bottom lip to stifle his groan as he poured himself inside her.

Rolling to the side, Sawyer tugged her limp body closer and spooned her.

"Mmm, this is the best way to go to sleep," she murmured. "I sleep best with you, big and warm, beside me."

At that sleepy murmur, she dropped off. Sawyer pressed his face to her hair. He liked knowing that she felt safe and happy with him in bed beside her.

He was falling for her.

He was falling in love with Hollis Stanton.

Closing his eyes, he pulled in a steadying breath. It had nothing to do with her acting skills or her fame. It was her confidence, her inner beauty, her quiet courage.

"I'll keep you safe. No matter what."

He dropped into a light sleep, but the vibration of his cellphone woke him. His internal body clock told him they'd only been in bed for an hour or so.

He grabbed the phone off the nightstand. *Fuck.* Someone had triggered the exterior cameras. On the screen, he saw two shadowy figures converging on the house in the darkness.

Fuck.

His mind focused instantly. He shook Hollis awake.

"What?" she mumbled sleepily.

"You need to get dressed."

Since they'd come to this cottage, he'd made her leave clothes and shoes out ready in case they needed to make a quick escape.

At his words, she shook sleep off fast. "They're here?"

"Someone's here. Get dressed, stay down, and be ready to move."

Sawyer quickly pulled his own clothes on, then opened the bedroom door. He let out a quiet whistle of a bird.

He saw Park move on the couch. Then his friend whistled back.

Sawyer grabbed his weapon and his small go bag packed with essentials. He pulled the backpack on.

Now, he needed to neutralize the threat and get Hollis to safety.

There was a sudden bang at the back of the house.

What the hell? He swiveled.

Park appeared. "They've set the house on fire."

Hell. "They're trying to flush us out."

They'd be waiting at the exits for them, guns in hand. He hadn't seen the third of Stankovic's team, but he'd be out there.

It didn't matter, because Sawyer was ready for them.

"Come on."

The three of them moved together, with Hollis safely tucked between Sawyer and Park. He knew she was afraid, but she followed his orders without hesitation.

Keeping low, they headed for the hallway.

"Down," Park said suddenly.

They dropped, and a flashlight beam shone through the windows. That was just like Park, sensing something just before it happened.

Sawyer watched the beam crisscross the room, but he was more focused on the crackle of flames at the back of the cottage.

They were caught in between them.

"Crawl." He tugged Hollis with him. They crawled down the hall and reached the tiny laundry room. Inside, Sawyer flicked the mat on the floor back. There was a trapdoor set into the floor that led to the crawlspace under the cottage.

Suddenly, gunfire sprayed the living room and glass shattered. Hollis muffled a scream.

"Guess they got sick of waiting," Park said.

"No patience," Sawyer added.

He dropped down through the trapdoor. Thankfully, there was a fair bit of room under the cottage, so he could fit easily. There were plenty of spiderwebs, too. He batted some away. Hollis followed right behind him, with Park bringing up the rear. They crawled to the edge of the cottage where some bushes grew thickly. Sawyer paused and listened.

There were two weapons firing at the front.

And... *There.*

Through the leaves of the shrub, he spotted another set of legs waiting at the back of the house. Sawyer lifted his handgun, then pressed his mouth to Hollis's ear. "Stay with Park."

She grabbed his hand. "Be careful. Please."

He nodded, and wished he had time to kiss her.

He stealthily moved out from under the house. Shadows were his old friends, and he used them to creep closer. All of his Ghost Ops training rushed back to him. How many missions had he been on like this? Creeping up on the enemy, his team at his side.

But now he had even more to fight for.

He advanced on the man. The guy was turned away from him, gaze focused on the house. The moonlight glinted off his bald head. Sawyer slid the gun away.

He'd do this quietly.

The man never saw or heard him.

Sawyer grabbed him from behind, pressing his forearm against the man's throat. He yanked the guy back, cutting off his air.

The hitman gurgled, and kicked his feet in the dirt. Sawyer held tight. This man had been trying to kill Hollis.

There would be no forgiveness.

It took a minute, but the man finally went slack. Sawyer dragged the body to the bushes and dumped him in the middle of them.

Then he hurried back to the house and crouched. "Clear."

Hollis scrambled out. Park followed her.

"Keep to the shadows under the trees," Sawyer said. "We're heading for the truck."

They needed to get away.

The three of them moved quickly. He felt Hollis grip the back of his shirt. They hadn't gone far when the assholes at the front of the cottage stopped firing.

Sawyer stopped, then tugged Hollis down. The three of them stayed crouched, and he scanned the area.

Two shadows stood at the front of the cottage. Dammit, they were standing between Sawyer and the truck.

"Branko, any sign of them?" one man yelled.

The fire broke through the roof with a loud noise. Sawyer felt Hollis jolt. Flames licked into the night sky.

"Branko?" the man called again.

"Shit, where is he?" the other man said with a heavy accent.

"Go and check."

Parker shifted. "I'll be back."

He melted into the darkness, and Sawyer pulled Hollis close.

"Branko? Goran?" The man out front cursed.

Sawyer smiled. Parker had taken out the second man. Ivan Stankovic wasn't a happy man.

As he watched, a shadow rose up behind the final hitman. Park wasted no time taking the man down.

There was a quick struggle, then it was over.

Park reappeared. "Let's go."

CHAPTER SIXTEEN

H ollis huddled in the backseat of the truck as Sawyer drove down the winding road.

She glanced back over her shoulder. "No one's following us."

"Let's hope it stays that way," Sawyer said.

She couldn't stop shaking. The hitmen had set fire to the cottage. She pressed a palm to her cheek. "I'm not worth all of this."

Sawyer met her gaze in the rearview mirror. "Yeah, you are."

Warmth bloomed in the cold filling her chest. She swallowed. "Where are we going?"

Parker sat silently in the passenger seat, texting on his phone. He looked up and the men shared a look. They had a silent way of communicating.

"The airport," Sawyer said.

"The airport." Hollis straightened. "Why?"

"The Norcross jet is still there," Parker said. "It's refueling now, and they're expecting us."

"We're leaving Maui?"

Sawyer nodded. "It's the safest option."

She wrapped her arms around herself. "And where will we go?"

"San Francisco. Vander will be waiting for us."

She leaned back against the seat. Okay, that didn't sound bad. They'd be far away from her would-be assassins. And they'd have reinforcements.

It would be much safer for Sawyer.

Lights pierced the dark night behind them. She glanced back and saw a car driving down the road. It wasn't speeding, but she leaned back, trying to get a better look. It was hard to see in the darkness. It looked like an older model car. She relaxed. It was probably just someone going somewhere in the middle of the night.

She'd just turned back to the front when she heard the roar of an engine. Suddenly, the car raced up beside them. A second later, it rammed into them.

Sawyer cursed.

Hollis gripped the seat. They were on a narrow stretch of road, flanked by trees on either side.

"Fucking hell," Park muttered.

The car rammed them again. Suddenly, two of their wheels were off the road, the truck shuddering. Sawyer gripped the steering wheel, fighting for control. The car rammed them a third time.

They hit something, then they were rolling.

Hollis screamed. Everything became a terrifying blur. Metal crunched and glass shattered.

They came to a stop, upside down, on the road. Her

heart was racing, and she tried to calm herself. *Oh, God. Oh, God. Oh, God.* She was hanging from her seat belt.

Deep breaths, Hols. She wasn't hurt, although she was sure she'd have a few aches and pains later.

"Sawyer?"

There was no answer and panic filled her throat.

"Sawyer? Are you all right?"

No answer.

"Park?"

She craned her head and saw Sawyer dangling from his seat belt. There was blood on his head. No. *No.*

"Park?" There was no response, and when she looked over, the front passenger seat was empty.

God, where was he? She fiddled with her seatbelt and unfastened it. She fell down awkwardly, and righted herself.

Then she heard footsteps. She froze. It was the driver of the other car. They were coming.

Fear shot through her.

She glanced over and saw the other door to the back-seat was cracked open. She slid across the seat, then nudged the door wider. She slid out and pressed her body against the side of the wrecked truck.

She had to help Sawyer.

As quietly as she could, she circled around the back of the truck. Crouching down, she carefully peered around.

The man walking toward the crashed truck was tall and lean. He had dark hair and a long face.

Gallant.

Her stomach contracted to a point. He was holding a gun.

"I just want the woman." He crouched at the driver's side and aimed the gun through the broken window.

Sawyer. She tensed. She had to do something.

"You don't need to die too," Gallant said.

No. No one was shooting her man. Fury exploded inside her. She was sick of being afraid and hunted.

And there was no way she was going to let Sawyer get killed.

She launched herself at the hitman.

Gallant's head jerked up, but he had no time to react before she was on him. She hit and scratched him.

"You asshole! I won't let you hurt him."

He made a sound, and she scratched his cheek. She kept slapping at his head.

Suddenly, she was pulled off him.

And into Sawyer's arms. Parker subdued the older man, forcing him down on his knees. He started zip tying Gallant's wrists together.

"Gorgeous, we had it covered," Sawyer said.

"What?" She clung to him. "He was going to hurt you."

"No, I was the bait. Park was ready."

"Oh... I..."

He smiled. "Protected me."

She felt heat in her cheeks. "Yes. You make good coffee, and you're a pretty decent pillow. I don't want to give that up."

He pulled her in for a hug. Hollis wrapped her arms around him and held on tight.

He was alive. He was okay.

She looked up. "Your head is bleeding." She touched his hair where the blood had matted it.

"Just a scratch, I promise."

Thank God. Hollis was starting to realize how much she needed this man. How much she needed him in her life.

"Who are you guys?" Gallant sounded annoyed. "This was supposed to be an easy job. A woman, alone. An actress with no training or skills."

No skills? Hollis felt like she should feel insulted.

Sawyer's body tensed. He carefully set her on her feet, then his hard gaze locked on the man on the ground. "You like killing innocent, defenseless women, Gallant?"

The hitman shrugged. "It's just business. It's not personal."

There was no emotion in his words. This was really just business. She shivered.

Sawyer strode up to him. "Well, this is personal to me. And my business is putting people like you behind bars." Sawyer crouched down and shot the man a cold smile. "But it's not personal."

Gallant sniffed. "I'm not the only one who took the contract. Nor were the idiot trio you took care of at the cottage."

Sawyer's mouth flattened. "How did you find us?"

"I followed them. They have a reputation for being able to ferret people out. They must have questioned someone."

"Anyone trying to get to her will have to go through me," Sawyer said darkly. "And my friend here."

The scary tone of his voice made her heart skip a beat.

The hitman stared at Sawyer for a beat, then glanced up at Park, before re-focusing on Sawyer. "You're not just a dinky Hawaiian deputy."

"No, he's not, motherfucker." Park yanked on the zip ties to tighten them.

The hitman winced.

"We're Ghost Ops," Sawyer said. "You picked the wrong job, buddy."

"Dammit," Gallant muttered. "This wasn't what I signed on for."

"Where's her bracelet?" Sawyer demanded.

The hitman sighed. "Back seat."

Sawyer strode over to the car and yanked the door open. He rummaged around inside, then came back holding her bracelet and her bottle of perfume.

Oh. She realized how sad she would have been to lose the bracelet Dave had given her.

Sawyer gripped her wrist, and clipped the bracelet on, then handed her the perfume.

"Thank you," she whispered.

He ran his fingers along her cheekbone, then his face hardened, and he looked at Parker. "Park, I need his keys."

Park fished around in Gallant's pocket, then tossed Sawyer the keys.

"Drag him behind the truck and secure his ankles. I'm going to message Jesse to come and get him, and take care of the others at the cottage."

173

"On it." Park gripped the back of Gallant's shirt. "Let's move, asshole."

"What are we doing now?" Hollis asked.

Sawyer strode over to the hitman's car. He held the back door open for her. "Continuing with our plan. We're getting off Maui."

She climbed into the back of the car. Soon, they were driving down the road toward Kahului in the hitman's vehicle.

She dozed off for a bit, but it was still dark when the car slowed. Hollis blinked awake, looking out the window. She saw the Kahului airport runway and the long, single-story main terminal in the distance. Sawyer pulled off onto a quiet side road. She saw a sign for helicopter tours and private aviation. They stopped in front of a large hangar.

Sawyer got out and opened the door for her. "Let's go, gorgeous."

She held his hand as they entered the hangar. The cavernous space was mostly empty, except for some tools and gear off to one side. They followed Park out the open hangar doors.

A sleek white jet stood on the tarmac, with its stairs lowered. Hollis had flown on private jets before, but it still always gave her a little thrill.

Battered and dirty, the three of them climbed aboard.

The pilot was a tall, older man, who stooped as he came out of the cockpit. He eyed them with a steady look, no shock or surprise on his face. "Rough night?"

"Yeah," Sawyer said.

The man nodded. "My name's Theo. There's a small restroom in the back, and a first aid kit in the galley."

Something told her that the Norcross pilot was used to people boarding his plane at all hours, looking rumpled and with blood on their clothes.

"Clean up and grab some food," Theo continued. "We'll be airborne shortly."

HOLLIS OPENED HER EYES. She heard the familiar drone of being on a plane.

She was warm and snug, and realized her head was resting on Sawyer's shoulder. A blanket had been tucked around her. She smiled. He'd tucked her in.

Sawyer had taken care of her more in the last week than anyone had in her entire life. She touched the bracelet on her wrist, rubbing her thumb on the silver links. She didn't just mean the big stuff of protecting her and saving her life. It was the small stuff too—feeding her, helping her relax, keeping her warm.

She saw he was dozing. Parker was asleep in the seat across the aisle.

Sawyer's eyes opened. God, she could look at that rugged face, and his green eyes flecked with gold, all day. The small cut near his hairline was barely visible. She'd cleaned it up earlier and washed away the blood.

"Hey," he said.

"Hey."

He took her hand. "You okay?"

She nodded, then looked out the window. Dawn was

starting to brand the sky with pink and gold, and down below, she saw the glimmer of city lights.

San Francisco.

"We'll be landing soon," he said.

She thought she'd feel better, safer, being away from Maui, but she still had a low-level churn in her belly.

This wasn't over. It wouldn't be until Michael Reuben was arrested, and assassins weren't trying to kill her anymore.

Parker came awake the same way Sawyer did. Asleep one minute, alert the next. "Anyone hungry?"

"Not me," Sawyer said.

Hollis shook her head. Her stomach was too full of knots for her to be able to eat anything.

Soon, the plane started its descent. The sun was well and truly up now, and she had a clear view of the Bay and the city. As they came in to land, she caught a glimpse of the iconic red-orange metal of the Golden Gate Bridge.

Parker was eating the food he'd made in the galley. The smell of the breakfast wrap made her feel queasy.

They landed and taxied toward a small private terminal, right on the water's edge. It was on the other side of the runway to the main terminal. Sawyer unbuckled his belt, and she followed him off the jet.

When they came down the steps, she saw two black BMW X6 SUVs waiting for them, and several men and one woman standing beside them.

They all had the look of people who could take care of themselves.

Hollis picked out Vander straight away. He wore a

blue suit and white shirt, with sunglasses hiding his eyes. That dangerous, intense vibe of his was even stronger in person.

She definitely didn't ever want to be on Vander Norcross' bad side.

"Vander." Sawyer greeted the other man, and they shared a hug, slapping each other on the back.

"Parker," Vander said.

Park gave Vander a chin lift, then they hugged as well.

Vander slid his sunglasses off and his dark eyes—that she now realized were actually dark blue—zeroed in on her.

"Hi," she said.

"Nice to meet you in person, Hollis. My wife wants an autograph, by the way."

A small laugh escaped her. "She can have as many autographs as she wants. I don't know how to thank you for everything you've done."

Vander cocked his head. "No thanks required. Now, our first priority is getting you back to Norcross Security."

That's when she turned her attention to the rest of his team. She realized that they were alert, and scanning around the area. Protecting them.

Protecting her.

She swallowed. "I'm safe here, right? No one knows I'm here?"

"I'm not a man who takes chances," Vander said.

Both Sawyer and Park made a sound.

Vander shook his head. "Fine, I only take chances when I know I can win." He turned and looked at his team. "Hollis, this is my second in command, Saxon Buchanan."

The blond man smiled at her. "A pleasure, Hollis."

"And this is my brother, Rhys," Vander said.

The dark-haired man shot her a charming smile. With his handsome face and tousled dark hair, he looked like a rockstar. "Love your movies."

"Thanks."

"And this is Siv Pedersen," Vander finished.

The tall, fit woman nodded. "Hello." Her voice held a touch of an accent.

"Let's move," Vander said. "We don't want Hollis out in the open."

They were ushered into the back of an SUV, and she found herself sandwiched between Sawyer and Park. It took them twenty minutes to arrive at a renovated warehouse on the edge of the city that housed the Norcross Security office. They drove into the lower level, the garage doors sliding closed behind them. More black X6s sat parked in a row.

"Nice digs," Park said.

"Down here is parking, the gym, and some holding rooms," Vander said. "Main offices are upstairs."

When Hollis stepped onto the main level, she took a second to take it all in. The industrial warehouse had been completely renovated. It was a huge open space with metal and glass, and a polished concrete floor. Original wooden beams and metal duct work crossed overhead.

Vander led her down the hall and into an office. The walls were a dark blue, and a glossy, black desk was topped with a laptop and a metal lamp. It was all sleek and sparse, so she couldn't read much from it. She guessed Vander Norcross only shared details about himself when he wanted to.

"Take a seat," Vander said.

Sawyer nudged her into one of the chairs in front of Vander's desk, then sat in the one beside her. Park leaned against the wall, while Vander leaned back against his desk and crossed his ankles.

"Hollis, this is Ace Oliveira."

She turned her head and saw a good-looking man standing in the doorway. He had a charming smile and his dark hair up in a messy man bun. He also had a baby girl strapped to his chest. She wore a pink, striped onesie, and a cute little hat on her head.

Hollis blinked. Did men know how seeing them with a cute baby added to their hotness factor?

Ace nodded at Park and Sawyer. "Hi, guys." Then he looked at Hollis. "Hi, Hollis. I'm a big fan. I loved your work in *Fatal Impact*."

"Thanks. And thanks for all the work you've done...to keep me breathing."

Ace rubbed the top of his baby's head. "I think Sawyer has done most of the hard work."

She looked at the man beside her. "He has. I wouldn't be here if it wasn't for him."

His face softened, and he gently gripped the back of her neck.

"I'm pretty sure I turned his quiet life upside down from the moment I set my coffee machine on fire," she said.

Ace's smile widened. "Sounds like there's a story there."

"It's been worth it," Sawyer said. "Every second."

His words seeped into her and took hold.

"Right." Vander sat behind his desk. "I know it's been a difficult and stressful few days."

Try terrifying few days.

"The FBI are planning to raid Reuben's house this morning, and take him into custody. They will tear his businesses apart, and put a stop to the flow of our weapons and technology to Russia."

Hollis blew out a breath. "Good."

"Once I get an update from my contact, I'll let you know. After lunch, we're going to take you to a secure apartment in Rincon Hill. It's not far from here. We use it when we have guests and clients here in the city. It's in a secure building, on the thirtieth floor. It's well appointed, and the kitchen is well-stocked. You'll be safe there until we can confirm that the contract on Hollis's life is void."

"It's almost over," she whispered.

Sawyer squeezed her hand. "You just have to hold on a little longer, gorgeous. I'll be with you every minute until then."

CHAPTER SEVENTEEN

S awyer led Hollis into the apartment. It was nice. Really nice. Vander had clearly spared no expense for his safehouse.

The first thing that caught the eye was the expansive view of the Bay and the Bay Bridge as it snaked across the water to Oakland. The view was showcased perfectly by the floor to ceiling windows.

"Oh, wow." Hollis walked past the long kitchen island and cream leather sofa. She stood at the windows, staring out over the water. The sun was setting in the opposite direction, but the growing shadows over the bay were still breathtaking.

"You must be tired," he said.

She turned and smiled, her red hair tangled around her face. "A little. It was a crazy night last night. Go to bed in Maui, escape killer assassins, and end up in San Franciso."

He wrapped his arms around her. "You did great. You didn't panic, didn't lose it."

She leaned into him. "There were a few moments where I wanted to, but knowing you were there, and Park, helped me keep my cool."

Sawyer pressed his mouth to hers and kissed her.

He felt so damn much for this woman. It somehow both scared the shit out of him, and made him happy.

"Why don't you take a shower?" he suggested. "Vander said we'll find some fresh clothes in the closet. I'll put some dinner together."

She nodded. "A shower sounds amazing."

"Leave your shoes at the door." He checked his SIG and set it on the kitchen island, along with his cellphone.

Her lips quirked. "You're always in protection mode."

He met her gaze. "When it comes to you, I am."

She toed off her shoes near the front door, then headed for the bedroom.

In the kitchen, Sawyer opened the fridge and pulled out some food. The apartment was done with touches of warm, sleek wood and cream-colored tiles. Modern light fixtures and bold artwork brightened the place up, and kept it from being plain.

Park was one floor up in a second apartment. Vander had dropped them off, assuring them that the building had good security.

"The floor below you is getting renovated, so there's no one close by," Vander said. "All the stairwells, the hallways, and the lobby have CCTV."

"Thanks, Vander," Sawyer said. "For everything. I owe you."

"I've always got your back, Sawyer. And your woman's."

Sawyer stared blindly at the food on the island, listening to the shower run down the hall.

His woman.

Yeah, that felt right. He started making some sandwiches. He realized that he wanted Hollis to be his. Forever.

Hell, he'd never thought he'd let someone that close. Put someone in the position where losing her could tear him apart. Thoughts of Tabish ran through him.

But could he give her up?

Hell, no.

There were obstacles, for sure. And risks. But Hollis was worth it. She was worth everything. They could make it work. A part of him had felt right with her, from the first moment he'd met her.

She wandered back into the kitchen wearing gray sweatpants and a T-shirt. Even in the casual clothes, she still managed to look beautiful.

"Ham and cheese sandwiches." He set a plate on the island. "And a glass of wine." He poured the white wine he'd found in the fridge into a glass.

She slipped onto one of the stools at the island. "One glass of wine and I'll be out," she warned.

Good. He wanted her to get some sleep.

On the island, his cellphone vibrated, and he glanced at the screen. "It's a message from Vander." Sawyer read it and his jaw tightened. "Damn."

"What's wrong?"

"The FBI can't find Reuben. They searched his home, offices, his studio, and other properties. No sign of him."

"God." She rested her fisted hand against her chest.

Sawyer circled the island. "It'll be okay. He can't hide forever. And now he's a risk to national security. That means he's on a lot of people's radars, and they won't stop until they find him."

She nodded, but there was worry on her face.

He pushed her hair to the side and kissed the back of her neck. "Trust me?"

"You know I do. More than anyone—"

The lights went out, plunging them into darkness.

"Oh, God," she said. "What's happening?"

His hands tightened on her. "I don't know. Maybe it's just a power outage." His instincts were screaming at him. His eyes adjusted to the city light filtering through the windows.

He wasn't going to take any chances with Hollis's life.

He felt around on the island and grabbed his cellphone and SIG. He pressed the phone screen and swore.

"Sawyer?"

"There's no signal."

"We're in the middle of San Francisco. How is that possible?"

"Someone's jamming it," he said grimly.

"What?" she gasped.

"Shoes on."

He pulled Hollis across the room, and she stumbled behind him. He slowed down and steadied her.

"I can't see a damn thing," she muttered.

"Don't worry, I have good night vision."

Her hand twisted in his T-shirt. "You think I have another hitman coming to kill me?"

"Possibly."

"That's just *great*."

He spun her and kissed her. He waited until her tense muscles relaxed and she melted against him. "Better?"

"Yes."

"We're leaving. Do everything I say."

She nodded. "Okay."

"Shoes on."

While she fumbled into her shoes, Sawyer's mind ticked over. He needed to get her out of there. He guessed the elevators weren't working, so they'd need to take the stairs.

When he reached out a hand to open the front door, that's when he realized it was ajar.

The hairs on the back of his neck rose. That could only mean one thing.

He spun and shoved Hollis to the side.

The man attacked, coming out of nowhere.

Their bodies collided. Sawyer's gun went flying. He slammed a punch toward the man's head. The guy was big, the same size as Sawyer, and he was fast. The asshole jerked his head to the side and rammed his own fist up. Sawyer blocked the blow. They traded several punches and shoves.

Fuck this. He hadn't used all of his skills in a long time.

But he would now.

For Hollis.

Sawyer rammed his elbow up in a vicious blow. Bone crunched and the man grunted. Sawyer followed through with two brutal jabs. Ribs cracked and the man made a pained sound.

It only took Sawyer seconds to disable the man. He dropped the unconscious man to the floor.

Chest heaving, he pulled in a breath.

He looked up and saw Hollis standing there, holding a vase over her head.

"I was going to help." She lowered it. "It looks like you didn't need it. That was..."

He waited for her to say something. For her to tell him it was brutal, horrible...

"Badass," she said.

His chest inflated. "Come on. This guy will have friends."

He took her hand, and they headed out into the hall. He searched for any movement in the darkness, but didn't sense anything. The thick carpet muffled their footsteps as they moved toward the stairwell. An emergency exit sign glowed in the darkness. He opened the door.

More low emergency lighting gave the stairwell an eerie glow.

"This reminds me of a movie where you *shouldn't* go down the stairs," Hollis whispered.

They had no choice.

"I'm not letting these assholes have you. Now, let's move."

COULD her life get anymore crappy?

Hollis couldn't believe she was hurrying down a scary stairwell in the dark with someone else out to kill her.

Sawyer's broad back was in front of her, the soft fabric of his T-shirt stretched over his hard muscles. He was her lifeline in all this craziness.

She was so glad he was with her. Once again, he was protecting her.

He stopped suddenly, and she caught herself before she ran into the back of him.

There was a bang of a door. It echoed from above. They both looked up, and Hollis heard voices—urgent and angry.

Sawyer muttered a curse, and grabbed her hand. He glanced around, then pushed open the door to the floor below their apartment.

Inside was thick darkness, and she struggled to see anything. As he started forward, she had to trust that he wouldn't let her trip over anything.

Sawyer held up his phone, and turned the flashlight function on.

Oh. The entire floor was open, dotted with pillars, construction tools, and drywall stacked in piles. It looked like someone was turning multiple apartments into one large place.

"Come on." He set off across the floor. She followed him, her eyes adjusting to the gloom of the city light filtering in through the windows.

They hadn't gone far when she heard voices behind them. *Oh, no.* Whoever was behind this had just entered the floor.

Sawyer extinguished the light and pulled her down behind...something. She thought it was a stack of bricks.

His warm lips pressed to her ear. "Quiet."

Like she planned to make any noise. Biting her lip, she waited. She heard the sounds of people moving in the darkness. They were talking to each other in low, hushed voices. In Russian.

She squeezed her eyes closed. Reuben. These guys had to belong to him. The sound of footsteps got closer. She tensed, fear trickling down her spine.

"Stay down," Sawyer murmured.

A man stepped right in front of them. She saw his dark boot.

Then Sawyer sprang up like a jaguar. *Thud. Thud.* Oh, man. Heart hammering in her throat, she listened to the vicious blows as he attacked. Someone grunted in pain, and she prayed it wasn't Sawyer. The pair were just a giant shadow as they whirled and wrestled with each other. She heard another man shout across the space.

Hollis bit her lip and felt around on the floor. Her hand closed over a brick.

Sawyer broke free and slammed a hard kick into his opponent's gut. The man flew back, tripping over a pile of tools.

Then the second man appeared out of the darkness, shouting in Russian, a gun aimed at Sawyer.

No. Emotions exploded inside her, her lungs locking. She couldn't lose this man. This good, honorable hero.

The newcomer stepped closer, right in front of her. He had no idea that she was crouched right at his knee.

He shouted again, and she knew that any second, he'd fire his weapon.

She leaped forward, swinging the brick. She crashed into him, the brick hitting his knee. He yelped and they both fell to the concrete floor. The gun went off.

Ears ringing, she tried to free herself. She was tangled up with the guy.

Then she was lifted free.

"Hollis? Are you hit?"

Sawyer's voice was sharp, urgent. She looked up into his angry face.

"I'm fine."

"What the *hell* were you doing?"

"Saving you."

He cocked his head. "I told you to stay hidden."

"I couldn't let him shoot you!"

More gunfire sounded from the other side of the floor.

Sawyer reacted before she could even think. He slammed into her, and they hit the dusty concrete floor. He moved into a crouch, then pulled her behind a stack of gear.

Bullets peppered around them.

"Dammit, there's a third attacker," he said. "We're pinned down. I wish I still had my damn gun." He patted around and lifted a hammer. "I'll distract him. You run to the next stack of gear. Keep your head down."

She nodded, throat tight. A hammer would be useless against a gun.

Sawyer rose on one knee, then tossed the hammer.

As more gunfire broke out, she ran, doubled over.

Bullets whizzed past nearby, and she cried out. She dived in behind some more gear, and felt skin rip off her elbow.

She heard more objects hitting the ground with a thud, and realized Sawyer was throwing more things at the attacker. The man kept firing.

Then all the noise stopped.

Eerie silence echoed around her. She couldn't hear anything, could barely see anything. What was happening?

Suddenly, a hand sank into her hair.

As Hollis was yanked upward, her hair pulling on her scalp, she cried out.

"Let me go!" she yelled.

The man with the gun had tattoos on his neck, and a scowl on his face. But as he looked at her, his lips curled into a smile. An ugly one.

Then Sawyer appeared, a gun aimed at the man. He must have grabbed one of the other attackers' weapons.

Her captor pulled her in front of him, like a shield.

"Stay back." The man had a thick Russian accent. "I will put a bullet in her head."

She felt the cold barrel of the gun press to her temple. Fear tried to choke her, but she tamped it down. She had to stay focused.

She met Sawyer's gaze.

The man behind her chuckled. "You have no options. Put down the gun."

"No," Sawyer growled.

"Do you want me to kill her?" He shook her.

"No."

The man made a scoffing sound. "You cannot stop me."

"Maybe I can't, but he can." Sawyer nodded.

Suddenly, her captor was yanked away. Hollis stumbled forward, and she heard the man's gun hit the floor.

She spun and saw Parker land a punch to the man's face. He followed through with some hard kicks and punches. The man dropped to his knees.

Thank God.

She turned and raced to Sawyer. He was already moving in her direction, and caught her against him.

"You're safe," he said against her hair.

"*Sawyer.*" She clung to him.

Overwhelming emotions welled up inside her.

She loved him. She was in love with Sawyer Lane.

She wanted to tell him, but before she could say anything, he tipped her chin up and kissed her.

CHAPTER EIGHTEEN

"This way." Sawyer waved Hollis and Parker down the stairwell.

The power was still off, and phones still jammed. There was no way of knowing if they'd neutralized all of the attackers who were after Hollis.

They headed for the cargo elevator. Sawyer wanted Hollis out of the building.

"You're sure the cargo elevator still had power?" Sawyer asked Park.

"Yep. Saw it myself when I was heading your way. It must be on a separate circuit."

A quick ride in the cargo elevator was better than getting caught in this stairwell.

"Stop," Park said suddenly.

Sawyer paused, and pulled Hollis close. He heard noises echo through the stairwell, but thankfully, they didn't sound too close.

"Sounds like a team is moving up the stairwell," Park murmured. After a second, he nodded.

Sawyer trusted the man's instincts. They'd saved Sawyer's life too many times to count.

Park opened the door to the next floor, and they moved into the hallway. They hurried past all the closed doors and finally reached the cargo elevator. It was tucked around the back of the floor, near the trash chutes.

The lights glowed on the panel.

Thank God. They deserved a break. Sawyer pressed the button. A minute later, the doors opened. It didn't have the fancy mirrored walls of the main elevators they'd used when they'd first arrived at the building. This elevator had simple metal walls.

They got inside, and Sawyer pressed the button for the ground floor.

"So, these guys are Russian," Park said.

Sawyer nodded. "Reuben's goons."

Hollis shivered, and Sawyer hugged her to his chest.

The elevator slowed, and he met Park's gaze. His friend nodded. They both shifted in front of Hollis, weapons in hand.

The doors opened into a maintenance area. It was dark and empty.

"Let's move." Sawyer took her arm. "Hollis, stay behind me."

Once again, they kept Hollis between them, and moved quietly. No attackers appeared.

They reached an exit door, and Sawyer cracked it open. It opened onto the sidewalk outside the building, and he checked in all directions. It was clear.

As they stepped outside, the night was cool, but not

cold. There was no one on the street, but a car drove past, paying no attention to them.

"Let's go," he said.

They hustled down the sidewalk. They crossed over the street, and Sawyer pulled out his phone. Suddenly, the signal clicked back in.

"We're outside the jammer's range." He stabbed at the screen.

Vander answered instantly. "Sawyer?"

"A team attacked the apartment. They cut off power to the building and jammed the phones. We just made it out."

Vander cursed.

"We're okay. They're Russian, Vander. It has to be Reuben."

"He's still in the wind and the FBI is pissed." Vander cursed again. "How the fuck did he find you?"

"No idea."

"We'll work that out later. Okay, I'm on my way. Stay where you are."

Hollis tugged on Sawyer's shirt. "Sawyer."

Her tone made him look up.

At the end of the block, several men rounded the corner of the building. They spotted them and started in their direction. They were just dark shadows, but they were big and moved like they had military training.

"Fuck, Vander, we have company. Track the location of my phone. We'll be on the move."

"I'm coming." There was a promise in his voice.

Vander had never once let Sawyer down.

He grabbed Hollis's hand, and broke into a jog. "Park, ideas?"

"No good ones."

Sawyer spotted an alley ahead. "There."

They sprinted down the narrow alley, and into the darkness. They passed a dumpster that reeked of rotting food. Sawyer towed Hollis behind him.

"They're coming." Park's voice was cool. He was in full battle mode.

"*Oh, God.*" There was no missing the fear in her voice.

"It's okay, gorgeous. I'm not letting anyone touch you."

"Here?" Park asked.

A nearby security light on one of the buildings offered a little bit of illumination. "Yeah. Like we did in Kamdesh?"

Park nodded.

Sawyer turned.

Hollis grabbed his arm. "Sawyer, we need to run—"

A gunshot rang out, and Hollis muffled a scream.

He put his body in front of hers. Four armed thugs were heading toward them. A shorter, rotund man stood in the center of them. They stopped, then the man stepped forward.

Sawyer recognized Michael Reuben.

Hollis sucked in a breath.

"Be brave," Sawyer whispered. "Trust me."

She swallowed and nodded.

"You have caused me a lot of problems, Ms. Stanton," Reuben said.

HOLLIS TOOK A HALF STEP FORWARD, staring at Reuben's face. He looked so...ordinary. Not like some criminal mastermind.

"This is all on you, Reuben," she said, rage welling inside her. "You're the criminal. Selling our tech and weapons to Russia."

The man's mouth tightened.

"Seriously, if you'd just left me alone, I never would have said anything."

Sawyer gripped her wrist, a warning.

But Hollis was done.

Done being chased and shot at. Done seeing Sawyer in danger. And Park, a man she barely knew, risking his life for her.

All because of this man standing in front of them.

"I barely heard anything that night at your house. I certainly had no evidence."

"I couldn't take that risk," Reuben said.

"I would have forgotten I heard anything if it wasn't for all the things that started happening. People following me, the car accident, the camera."

"My work is too important. I won't let anything stop me." Reuben glanced at Sawyer and Park. "Your guard dogs can't save you this time."

Sawyer made a sound. "You're going to be very disappointed, Reuben. Or should I say Mikhail?"

"It ends here," Reuben said. "Nothing will stop my work to support my home country. My *real* country."

One of the men beside Reuben stepped forward and

holding a knife. Hollis sucked in a breath. It was the bodyguard who'd spotted her in his house. Scarface. She saw the puckered scar on his cheek.

He flicked the knife open, then closed. Open, then closed. His gaze was on her like a snake, waiting to strike. She glared back at him.

"It's already over," Sawyer said. "The FBI raided your home and businesses today. I'm surprised you haven't heard."

Reuben's eyes widened, and Hollis felt a spurt of satisfaction.

"*No,*" the older man breathed. "You're lying."

"Look it up," Sawyer said. "They know about your shipments. You're a wanted man."

Reuben yanked out his cellphone. "Keep your guns on them." He scrolled through the phone, then let out an enraged sound.

Hollis smiled. He was a man used to doing what he wanted, when he wanted. All that was coming to an end.

Reuben's head snapped up. "You bitch. You stupid, airhead actress."

"I'm not an airhead, asshole. And I'm an excellent actress."

"You're trash," he spat. "I looked into your background. You're one step from the trailer park. You're *nothing*. I won't let a nothing like you ruin everything." His voice echoed in the alley.

"I am *not* nothing. I'm the woman I've made myself to be. Being born poor and disadvantaged wasn't my choice or my fault. And it's not some stain to carry around. Anyone can change their circumstances, and be what they want to be. It's a shame that you chose to be a lying, scheming terrorist."

There was enough light that she could see Reuben's face turning red, and the look of hatred he aimed her way.

"For decades I've put plans in place, and in just a few seconds of eavesdropping, you destroyed it all."

Sawyer tensed beside her, watching Reuben carefully.

He was like a bomb, ready to detonate.

"You deserved it," Hollis said. "I'm glad I overheard you." She didn't love having people trying to kill her, but because of Reuben, she'd met Sawyer. And now, Reuben would be stopped. "You're going down, and you'll spend the rest of your life rotting in prison."

Reuben let out an angry roar, then spat out a word in Russian.

It all happened so fast. Scarface took a step forward, his arm moving.

Sawyer leaped in front of her, and his body jerked.

What? What had happened?

Suddenly, Parker fired, gun swiveling. *Bam. Bam. Bam.*

Sawyer dragged her down to the ground, and she saw two guards fall. The other was turning, and Scarface was reaching for another weapon.

Even more gunfire echoed in the alley, and Hollis cried out.

Then silence.

She lifted her head. Reuben stood there, staring in

horror. His men were all lying on the ground around him. None of them were moving.

Boots clicked on the concrete, and several shadows emerged from the mouth of the alley.

"You've made a lot of bad choices, Reuben. Your number one mistake was coming to my city and targeting my friends."

Vander Norcross stood there, hands by his sides.

Flanking him were Saxon, Siv, Rhys, and a tall African American man Hollis recognized as Rome Nash. They all had weapons in their hands.

"Good timing," Sawyer said.

"Thank God," Hollis said shakily.

"Secure them," Vander ordered. "The FBI are on their way."

Rhys Norcross yanked Reuben's arms behind his back and cuffed him.

It was finally over.

Hollis blinked, not quite believing it. "Sawyer, Reuben is done. It's over." She shifted on the ground, turning his way. Then her blood ran cold.

"Oh my God. *Sawyer*." She stared at the blood on his shirt.

"I'm okay."

She shook her head. "That is an incredibly man thing to say when you have a *knife* stuck in your chest." Her voice rose to a high pitch. Panic and fear flooded her. The knife was buried in the top of his right pec, blood turning his shirt red.

She gripped his arm and saw that his face was pale. He was trying to hide the fact that he was in pain.

Vander knelt beside them. "Ouch."

"It'll be fine." Sawyer scowled. "It didn't hit anything vital."

"Better leave it in," Vander suggested. "Just in case."

"How do you know it didn't hit anything vital?" Hollis said. "Do you have a medical degree?"

"Hey." Sawyer cupped her cheek. "Take a deep breath, gorgeous. I'll be all right."

She gripped his wrist. "Sawyer, I can't lose you."

"Not going to happen." He pulled her closer and pressed his forehead to hers. "I'm not going anywhere."

CHAPTER NINETEEN

He barely paid any attention to Vander and his team corralling Reuben and his goons.

Sawyer was focused solely on Hollis.

Worry lined her face, and she kept touching him, her hands shaking. Her gaze was locked on his bloody shoulder and the knife still piercing his skin.

"I'm really going to be okay," he told her.

"You got stabbed, and it's all my fault."

"Don't say that," he growled. "It's Reuben's fault. And I'd take a hundred knives to protect you."

Her teeth sank into her bottom lip.

"I'm not leaving you," he murmured. "If you give me the chance, I'll never leave you."

Her beautiful blue eyes widened, and her lips parted.

This felt like the biggest risk he'd ever taken. He'd leaped from planes, been in too many firefights to count, gone on the most dangerous missions, but this moment felt the scariest.

"You...live in Maui," she said. "I live in LA."

"Hollis, I don't care about geography." He dragged in a deep breath. "I love you."

The air shuddered out of her. "You do?"

In those quiet words, he heard the little girl who'd just wanted to be loved. Who'd been let down by so many people.

"I do. I don't care about your movies or Oscars, I love *you.*"

"Really?" she whispered.

"You ever known me to lie?"

"Never. You're the best, most honest man I've ever met." She dragged in a deep breath. "I love you too, Sawyer. So much it terrifies me."

She loved him. Hell. He felt lightheaded. He pulled her closer. "You don't need to be afraid. I'll always protect you, care for you, and love and adore you."

"*Sawyer...*"

He kissed her, and he tasted salt. He realized tears were streaming down her face.

Suddenly, she jerked back. "Oh God, your injury."

"Don't worry. I'm sure Vander's got a good first aid kit at the office."

"What?" Her eyes went wide. "No way, Sawyer Lane. You're going to the hospital. What if you have internal bleeding? What if you've cut a tendon or something? I am *not* losing you. We're going to the hospital."

"Ambulance is on the way," Vander said from nearby.

"Aw, hell," Sawyer complained. But he wanted to put Hollis at ease. If going to the hospital did that, he'd go.

"If you love me, you'll do this," she said. "Please."

202

He twined his fingers with hers. "I'd do anything for you."

"I know. You've shown me that from the moment we first met." She pressed a kiss to his mouth, then nibbled on his lip. "I love my work, and I know that you love yours and Maui. How will we make this work?"

"We'll work it out, I promise. Because it's worth the effort."

She nodded. "And you always keep your promises."

He heard sirens, and a few moments later, several black SUVs, police cars, and an ambulance turned into the alley.

Hollis didn't leave his side as the paramedics checked him over. She didn't even watch as Reuben and his men got shoved into the FBI vehicles.

He got strapped to a gurney and settled into the ambulance. Hollis sat beside him, holding his hand.

"We'll meet you at the hospital," Vander told them. Bedside him, Park gave them a salute.

Sawyer nodded, and watched as Vander closed the ambulance doors.

"It's really over now," she murmured.

"This mess is over." He rubbed the smooth skin on her wrist, right beside her bracelet. "But we're just getting started."

She smiled, but then she looked down at his bloody shirt. "After you get to the hospital, and don't have a knife sticking out of you anymore."

As the ambulance pulled away, the paramedic in the back with them turned to look at her. "Hey, are you...?"

"I am, but please focus on the love of my life. I don't want him bleeding to death."

With a nod, the paramedic set to work checking Sawyer's vitals. "Not going to let that happen, Ms. Stanton."

Right then, Sawyer felt a little grateful to Michael Reuben. Not about the knife wound, but for bringing Hollis into his life.

He met her gaze.

She'd woken him up, and now, he was never letting her go.

"CAREFUL." Hollis held Sawyer's hand as they headed down the hospital corridor.

"Gorgeous, I'm fine. I'm all bandaged up and the doctor cleared me."

The knife was gone, and he'd been stitched up. Sawyer had been right, and the knife hadn't hit anything vital. The sense of relief she felt was immense.

"I also heard him say that you'd lost a lot of blood, and need to hydrate and rest."

Sawyer stopped and pulled her to his chest. "I'm *fine*. And I'll rest, with you."

She smiled, her heart squeezing. God, she was totally in love with this man.

He dropped a kiss to her nose.

"Come on," she said. "Vander's bringing the SUV around the front."

The hospital doors opened, and as they stepped outside, they were blinded by pops of light.

Then the shouts started.

"Hollis, who's the man?"

"Hollis, can you confirm that you were involved in an altercation in Rincon Hill?"

"Hollis, over here!"

She turned away from the crowd of people with cameras.

"Vultures," she muttered.

"It's okay." He squeezed her hand.

She lifted her head. "No, it's not. You'll be on all the entertainment news programs, magazines, websites. They'll dig into your life."

He shrugged. "I don't care. You're worth it."

For a second, her chest was so tight she couldn't breathe. She'd never been worth it to anyone before. "I love you."

The corner of his lips lifted. "I know."

She turned to the crowd and squared her shoulders. "I'll issue a press release soon through my agent, Tavion Hall. For now, I just want to get home with the man I love, who saved my life, so he can rest."

There was a wild explosion of more shouts and questions.

Hollis turned away from them. Let them chew on that. She wasn't giving them anything else.

A car horn honked. Then someone laid on the horn and the crowd shifted. An X6 pulled to a stop in front of them.

Vander got out, circled around, and opened the back door for them.

"That's Vander Norcross," someone in the crowd said.

There were more excited whispers. Vander ignored them all.

Hollis climbed in, and Sawyer sat beside her. A heartbeat later, Vander slid into the driver's seat, and they were off.

"How many stitches?" Vander asked.

"Only seven," Sawyer replied.

Vander made a sound. "I got twenty once."

Sawyer snorted. "That's nothing. I got thirty-three."

Vander nodded. "I remember that. You didn't move fast enough."

Hollis rolled her eyes. "This is not a competition."

Sawyer grinned, and he looked younger and more relaxed than he had in a long time.

This amazing man loved her. That left her feeling giddy.

"I found out how Reuben found you guys. A damn baggage handler at the private terminal at the airport spotted Hollis when you guys landed. He posted a pic on social media."

She grimaced. "Welcome to my life."

Sawyer eyed Vander. "Something tells me that baggage handler doesn't have a job anymore."

"No, he does not," Vander said.

Vander drove them to the Norcross Security office. The lights on the main level were off, but on the top floor, she saw that some lights were on.

"I live above the office," Vander told her. "You'll stay with us for the night, or what's left of it."

They parked in the garage and Hollis leaned into Sawyer's side as they headed upstairs. Vander didn't stop on the main level. He led them to a private elevator.

When they reached the top, a woman stood on the landing, waiting for them.

She was a few inches shorter than Hollis, with a fit body, and brown hair pulled back in a ponytail. Sharp, pale-blue eyes took them in.

"Hi, Hollis, I'm Brynn Norcross. I'm a huge fan."

Hollis got the impression of intelligence and confidence. A woman who could handle herself.

"Sorry to disrupt your night."

Brynn smiled and threw her husband an amused smile. "Don't worry, we're used to that around here."

She held out a hand and Hollis shook it.

The woman's blue gaze switched to Sawyer. "How many stitches?"

"Seven."

Brynn gave him a quick hug. "Pfft, that's nothing. I had fifteen once."

Hollis blinked.

"I'm a police detective. Come in." Brynn stepped back and waved them inside.

Their place had the same industrial vibe as the office below. There were wooden floors and touches of black iron. A wall of accordion doors, currently closed, led onto a roof terrace. Beyond it, the buildings of the city speared up, offering a fabulous view.

Dragging her gaze off the terrace, Hollis noticed

Parker sitting at the kitchen island, cradling a steaming mug.

"Hey," Park said. "Only seven stitches, huh? That's barely a scratch."

Hollis glared at him. "I don't want to know how many stitches you've had in the past. He took a knife for me."

Sawyer ran a hand over her back. "She's still a bit tense."

"I'll make you some herbal tea, Hollis," Brynn said. "It sounds gross, but we have some good ones."

"I'll help you." She shot Sawyer a look. "Sit."

She waited until he sank onto the black leather couch before she followed Brynn to the kitchen.

There was a loud *woof*. A dog appeared. It was a Belgian Malinois, with a black face and ears, and a tan-colored body.

It raced to Brynn for a pat, then the dog made a beeline for Vander. The man ran his hand along the dog's back.

"This is Shadow."

"Hi, Shadow," Hollis said. She'd always wanted a dog growing up.

The dog, who didn't look much past the pup stage, headed toward her and nudged her with his nose, his tail wagging.

Then, he headed for the couch.

"Good looking dog," Sawyer said.

Brynn smiled. "We sort of accidentally adopted him."

Soon, Shadow was snuggled into Sawyer's uninjured side on the couch.

While Brynn and Hollis made tea, Vander poured

bourbon for the men. "Eagle Rare," Vander said. "The 17-year-old."

"His favorite," Brynn added.

"I'm in," Park said.

"Me too," Sawyer said.

"Hey, you're on painkillers," Hollis reminded him.

"I think I've earned a bourbon."

After the drinks were poured, Vander sat in an armchair, with Brynn resting on the arm. Parker sat on the other end of the couch. Hollis sat beside Sawyer, Shadow lying between them.

"Well done on a successful mission." Vander lifted his glass.

Parker and Sawyer held their glasses up as well.

"It was the most important one I've ever been on." Sawyer met her gaze, and she felt a flush of warmth.

Then Sawyer looked over at Vander. "I get it now."

Vander smiled and tugged his wife closer. "Good."

"I've got a flight back to Alaska tomorrow morning," Parker announced.

"Already?" Hollis said.

He nodded.

She realized that she'd miss him. "Thank you, Park. For everything."

He gave her a faint smile. "Thanks for not caving my head in with a frying pan."

She smiled. From the look on Sawyer's face, she realized that he'd miss his friend, too.

"You don't need to leave so soon, Park," Vander said. "Why don't you stay a few days."

"I...need to get back."

Vander eyed him for a second, then nodded. "You need anything from me, I'm here for you."

"Me too," Sawyer said.

Park looked at his boots for a second, then lifted his gaze. "I know."

The men continued talking, and soon, Hollis could barely keep her eyes open.

"Time for bed, sleeping beauty," Sawyer murmured.

"Is that an order, Deputy Lane?"

His eyes fired. "It is. I'll always look after you. No matter what."

CHAPTER TWENTY

Hollis blew out a breath, leaned down, and felt the stretch.

God, she felt good. The sun was shining, the waves were lapping the shore, and she was doing yoga by the pool.

It had been three weeks since Reuben had been arrested. She and Sawyer had stayed in San Francisco until they'd had confirmation that the contract on her life had been rescinded.

Apparently, hitmen didn't like doing jobs where they didn't get paid.

Still holding her downward dog, she glanced at her watch. Sawyer would be home from work soon. Tonight, she was finally cooking him her world-famous pepper steak stir fry.

She rose and stretched her arms up to the sky, and moved into the eagle pose. They'd mostly stayed here at Archer's place, and only spent the odd night at Sawyer's cottage. She was keeping busy reading the scripts that

Tavion sent her. Tave had been ecstatic when she'd finally called him to let him know she was safe.

She eyed the script resting on the nearby pool lounger. It was the Lehman script. The Western saga. She really liked this one. She wanted to do it. Nerves took flight in her belly.

It was going to suck to leave Sawyer.

She'd gotten used to cooking with him, lying on the couch snuggling together, sleeping beside him.

Loving him.

Every night now, he slept soundly beside her.

Her balance wobbled. She lowered her arms and legs. She wanted to do the job that she loved, but she also wanted Sawyer.

She heard the sliding door open and spun. She watched him step out of the house.

He was in his uniform. A hot shiver ran through her. She *loved* him in uniform. A couple of times in the bedroom, they'd played deputy and misbehaving criminal, much to her delight.

Her deputy liked to spank her when she was naughty.

"Hey there," she said.

He smiled. "Hi." His gaze ran appreciatively over her yoga leggings and top.

"Did you have a good day?" she asked.

"Yes, but it's better now." He wrapped an arm around her waist and kissed her.

A sense of rightness filled her. She was where she was supposed to be.

So how was she going to leave him?

He glanced down at the script. "How's this one?"

"Good. Really good."

"You want me to read it?"

She nodded. He'd been reading her scripts, and offering excellent feedback. She liked bouncing ideas off him.

He slid his hand into her hair. "You're awfully tense for someone doing yoga."

"I'm fine." She dredged up a smile. "I'm going to make you my pepper steak stir fry."

"Hollis." He paused, his gaze on her face. "You want to take this role."

"Yes." She pulled away. "But there will be shoots on the mainland, and at several locations in Europe. I'll be gone for months." Tears welled in her eyes. "We'll barely see each other."

She'd found her happy. She'd found the man she loved and who loved her back. And he didn't just say the words, he showed her with his actions.

Why did she have to choose between the two things that fed her soul, that completed her?

"Hey." He gripped her shoulders. "I told you that we'd work this out."

"I know, but your home and job are here."

"It's your home now, too."

Maui had become home. She loved the ocean, she loved Paia, and adored his friends and family. They treated her like a normal person.

Yes, this was home. Mostly thanks to this man.

"But I love my work as well." Her face crumpled.

He pulled her against his chest. "No crying. I have a

solution. I'm coming with you on your shoot. As your security."

Her head shot up. "What?"

"I'm coming with you. There is no way we're spending months apart."

"But Sawyer, your work—"

"I already have a plan. I've been talking with Jesse. He'd like to spend more time with his grandkids, and help his son in his restaurant. But he's not quite ready to retire yet."

Her brow creased. "I don't understand."

"We're going to share the job. We'll both work part-time, around your schedule."

Her mouth dropped open.

He rubbed his thumb over her lip. "I've got money saved up. I didn't spend much when I was in the military, and I invested well. So, it won't be a financial hit. I don't spend a lot anyway."

Her pulse pounded in her ears, excitement growing in her belly. "And as my private security, I'll pay for flights and accommodation while we're away."

"Deal."

Happiness swamped her. "Oh my God, you're coming with me!" She leaped on him, clamping her legs around his waist. "And in between movies, we'll come back here to Maui. To Paia. To home."

"Sounds perfect," he said, his hands sliding under her ass.

She smacked a kiss to his lips. "More than perfect. Sawyer, I had no idea that I could be this happy."

"Believe it, gorgeous. I'm planning to work hard to make you happy for the rest of our lives."

Several months later

SAWYER OPENED THE LIMOUSINE DOOR, ignoring the flashes from the cameras and screams from the crowd. He eyed the bystanders behind the barricades, and saw that the security team was doing a good job with crowd control.

He held out a hand to Hollis. She put her hand in his and stepped out of the limousine.

Damn, she looked amazing. She wore a long column of midnight-blue silk that skimmed her body lovingly. Her red hair was out and in loose waves.

He leaned down. "You take my breath away."

She smiled and there were more camera flashes. "You say that when I'm on the couch wearing my sweatpants."

"It's true then as well."

"I love you." She straightened his bow tie. "And I cannot believe how hot you look in a tuxedo." She went up on her toes and pressed a quick kiss to his mouth that set the crowd of fans off. "I'm *very* excited to take it off you later."

His cock twitched and he fought for some control. The last thing he needed in front of this crowd was a hard on. He resisted the urge to swat her ass. "Later. Come on, we have a movie premiere to attend."

She slid her arm through his and they started down

the red carpet toward the iconic Grauman's Chinese Theater.

She stopped for a second and waved to the fans, a huge, glamorous smile on her face.

She was his.

This Hollis—the glossy movie star—and the real Hollis underneath—the one who'd been battered by life, but never gave up—were both his.

She turned her smile on him, and they continued down the red carpet.

"About time you two arrived." Tavion appeared, looking sharp in his burgundy tuxedo jacket. Hollis's agent had his dark hair cut short and his goatee trimmed to perfection.

"Tave," Sawyer said.

"Sawyer."

Much to Hollis's delight, he and her agent had become fast friends. They both loved football and had been to several games together.

"Red, you look gorgeous." Tave kissed her cheek.

"You look devastatingly handsome. As always."

He flashed her a smile. "I think your lawman gives you a certain glow."

She beamed up at Sawyer. "He does."

"I read today that you're pregnant with triplets," Tave said.

She rolled her eyes. "It was twins last week."

Tave smiled. "As long as when you two really do reproduce, I get to be the baby's very stylish godfather." He squeezed her arm. "I'll see you both inside."

As he strode off, Hollis turned back to Sawyer.

"God, you're handsome," she said.

He snorted. "I am *never* wearing a burgundy jacket."

"All right." She glanced around. "Tave didn't notice. Think anyone has?" She nodded at her hand.

An ice-white diamond rested on her finger. The oval-shaped diamond he'd picked for her rested on a platinum band.

"Not yet." The screams would be deafening if anyone had noticed.

He'd proposed on the last day filming in Budapest. He'd rented a boat for a night cruise on the Danube. They'd eaten, laughed, watched the sights of the city float past. When he'd gotten down on one knee, she'd cried, laughed, and said yes. Very enthusiastically.

It had been the best moment of his life. Well, maybe tied with rescuing a gorgeous, redheaded actress in the act of trying to turn a smoke alarm off.

They'd had a good time over the months they'd traveled for the filming of her movie. He'd never realized how grueling the work could be, or how much fun they'd have. Quickies in her trailer were a special favorite of his.

Hollis had joked about setting a goal to make love in every country around the world. As much as he loved the idea, he'd been to some countries that he'd never take her to.

But in the rest of them, he was more than happy to get naked for her.

During the filming, they'd snuck off whenever they could for romantic dinners and sightseeing strolls. Best of all, he'd slept beside her every night. His nightmares weren't completely gone, but they didn't come as frequently anymore.

There had been a stalker for him to deal with in Paris. The man was now behind bars, but Sawyer was certain that the little chat he'd had with the man before the police had taken him away had set him straight.

Sawyer would always be there for her, protecting and loving her. They were making their life together, their way. After this premiere, they would fly back to Maui for some much needed downtime.

She leaned into him. "There is nowhere else I'd rather be, Deputy Lane, than with you. Thank you for being mine."

"That's one thing you never need to thank me for."

Love shone in her blue eyes.

As long as he was by Hollis's side, he was happy. He knew that he was exactly where he was meant to be.

He tucked his fiancée closer to his side and they walked inside.

I hope you enjoyed Sawyer and Hollis' story!

Unbroken Heroes continues with *The Hero She Loves*, starring loner Parker Conroy. Coming January 2025.

If you'd like to know more about **Vander Norcross** and his team, then check out the first Norcross Security book, *The Investigator,* starring Rhys Norcross. **Read on for a preview of the first chapter.**

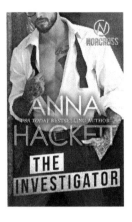

Don't miss out! For updates about new releases, free books, and other fun stuff, sign up for my VIP mailing list and get your *free box set* containing three action-packed romances.

Visit here to get started: www.annahackett.com

Would you like a FREE BOX SET of my books?

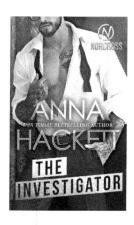

There was a glass of chardonnay with her name on it waiting for her at home.

Haven McKinney smiled. The museum was closed, and she was *done* for the day.

As she walked across the East gallery of the Hutton Museum, her heels clicked on the marble floor.

God, she loved the place. The creamy marble that made up the flooring and wrapped around the grand pillars was gorgeous. It had that hushed air of grandeur that made her heart squeeze a little every time she stepped inside. But more than that, the amazing art the Hutton housed sang to the art lover in her blood.

Snagging a job here as the curator six months ago had been a dream come true. She'd been at a low point in her life. Very low. Haven swallowed a snort and circled a stunning white-marble sculpture of a naked, reclining woman with the most perfect resting bitch face. She'd never guessed that her life would come crashing down at age twenty-nine.

She lifted her chin. Miami was her past. The Hutton and San Francisco were her future. No more throwing caution to the wind. She had a plan, and she was sticking to it.

She paused in front of a stunning exhibit of traditional Chinese painting and calligraphy. It was one of their newer exhibits, and had been Haven's brainchild. Nearby, an interactive display was partially assembled. Over the next few days, her staff would finish the installation. Excitement zipped through Haven. She couldn't wait to have the touchscreens operational. It was her passion to make art more accessible, especially to children. To help them be a part of it, not just look at it. To learn, to feel, to enjoy.

Art had helped her through some of the toughest times in her life, and she wanted to share that with others.

She looked at the gorgeous old paintings again. One portrayed a mountainous landscape with beautiful maple trees. It soothed her nerves.

Wine would soothe her nerves, as well. *Right.* She

needed to get upstairs to her office and grab her handbag, then get an Uber home.

Her cell phone rang and she unclipped it from the lanyard she wore at the museum. "Hello?"

"Change of plans, girlfriend," a smoky female voice said. "Let's go out and celebrate being gorgeous, successful, and single. I'm done at the office, and believe me, it has been a *grueling* day."

Haven smiled at her new best friend. She'd met Gia Norcross when she joined the Hutton. Gia's wealthy brother, Easton Norcross, owned the museum, and was Haven's boss. The museum was just a small asset in the businessman's empire. Haven suspected Easton owned at least a third of San Francisco. Maybe half.

She liked and respected her boss. Easton could be tough, but he valued her opinions. And she loved his bossy, take-charge, energetic sister. Gia ran a highly successful PR firm in the city, and did all the PR and advertising for the Hutton. They'd met not long after Haven had started work at the museum.

After their first meeting, Gia had dragged Haven out to her favorite restaurant and bar, and the rest was history.

"I guess making people's Instagram look pretty and not staged is hard work," Haven said with a grin.

"Bitch." Gia laughed. "God, I had a meeting with a businessman caught in...well, let's just say he and his assistant were *not* taking notes on the boardroom table."

Haven felt an old, unwelcome memory rise up. She mentally stomped it down. "I don't feel sorry for the cheating asshole, I feel sorry for whatever poor shmuck got more than they were paid for when they walked into the boardroom."

"Actually, it was the cheating businessman's wife."

"Uh-oh."

"And the assistant was male," Gia added.

"Double uh-oh."

"Then said cheater comes to my PR firm, telling me to clean up his mess, because he's thinking he might run for governor one day. I mean, I'm good, but I can't wrangle miracles."

Haven suspected that Gia had verbally eviscerated the man and sent him on his way. Gia Norcross had a sharp tongue, and wasn't afraid to use it.

"So, grueling day and I need alcohol. I'll meet you at ONE65, and the first drink is on me."

"I'm pretty wiped, Gia—"

"Uh-uh, no excuses. I'll see you in an hour." And with that, Gia was gone.

Haven clipped her phone to her lanyard. Well, it looked like she was having that chardonnay at ONE65, the six-story, French dining experience Gia loved. Each level offered something different, from patisserie, to bistro and grill, to bar and lounge.

Haven walked into the museum's main gallery, and her blood pressure dropped to a more normal level. It was her favorite space in the museum. The smell of wood, the gorgeous lights gleaming overhead, and the amazing paintings combined to create a soothing room. She smoothed her hands down her fitted, black skirt. Haven was tall, at five foot eight, and curvy, just like her mom had been. Her boobs, currently covered by a cute, white blouse with a tie around her neck, weren't much to write home about, but she had to buy her skirts one size bigger. She sighed. No matter how much she walked or jogged —*blergh*, okay, she didn't jog much—she still had an ass.

Even in her last couple of months in Miami, when stress had caused her to lose a bunch of weight due to everything going on, her ass hadn't budged.

Memories of Miami—and her douchebag-of-epic-proportions-ex—threatened, churning like storm clouds on the horizon.

Nope. She locked those thoughts down. She was *not* going there.

She had a plan, and the number one thing for taking back and rebuilding her life was *no* men. She'd sworn off anyone with a Y chromosome.

She didn't need one, didn't want one, she was D-O-N-E, done.

She stopped in front of the museum's star attraction. Claude Monet's *Water Lilies*.

Haven loved the impressionist's work. She loved the colors, the delicate strokes. This one depicted water lilies and lily pads floating on a gentle pond. His paintings always made an impact, and had a haunting, yet soothing feel to them.

It was also worth just over a hundred million dollars.

The price tag still made her heart flutter. She'd put a business case to Easton, and they'd purchased the painting three weeks ago at auction. Haven had planned out the display down to the rivets used on the wood. She'd thrown herself into the project.

Gia had put together a killer marketing campaign,

and Haven had reluctantly been interviewed by the local paper. But it had paid off. Ticket sales to the museum were up, and everyone wanted to see *Water Lilies*.

Footsteps echoed through the empty museum, and she turned to see a uniformed security guard appear in the doorway.

"Ms. McKinney?"

"Yes, David? I was just getting ready to leave."

"Sorry to delay you. There's a delivery truck at the back entrance. They say they have a delivery of a Zadkine bronze."

Haven frowned, running through the next day's schedule in her head. "That's due tomorrow."

"It sounds like they had some other deliveries nearby and thought they'd squeeze it in."

She glanced at her slim, silver wristwatch, fighting back annoyance. She'd had a long day, and now she'd be late to meet Gia. "Fine. Have them bring it in."

With a nod, David disappeared. Haven pulled out her phone and quickly fired off a text to warn Gia that she'd be late. Then Haven headed up to her office, and checked her notes for tomorrow. She had several calls to make to chase down some pieces for a new exhibit she wanted to launch in the winter. There were some restoration quotes to go over, and a charity gala for her art charity to plan. She needed to get down into the storage rooms and see if there was anything they could cycle out and put on display.

God, she loved her job. Not many people would get excited about digging around in dusty storage rooms, but Haven couldn't wait.

She made sure her laptop was off and grabbed her handbag. She slipped her lanyard off and stuffed her phone in her bag.

When she reached the bottom of the stairs, she heard a strange noise from the gallery. A muffled pop, then a thump.

Frowning, she took one step toward the gallery.

Suddenly, David staggered through the doorway, a splotch of red on his shirt.

Haven's pulse spiked. *Oh God, was that blood?* "David—"

"Run." He collapsed to the floor.

Fear choking her, she kicked off her heels and spun. She had to get help.

But she'd only taken two steps when a hand sank into her hair, pulling her neat twist loose, and sending her brown hair cascading over her shoulders.

"Let me go!"

She was dragged into the main gallery, and when she lifted her head, her gut churned.

Five men dressed in black, all wearing balaclavas, stood in a small group.

No...oh, no.

Their other guard, Gus, stood with his hands in the air. He was older, former military. She was shoved closer toward him.

"Ms. McKinney, you okay?" Gus asked.

She managed a nod. "They shot David."

"I kn—"

"No talking," one man growled.

Haven lifted her chin. "What do you want?" There was a slight quaver in her voice.

The man who'd grabbed her glared. His cold, blue eyes glittered through the slits in his balaclava. Then he ignored her, and with the others, they turned to face the *Water Lilies*.

Haven's stomach dropped. *No.* This couldn't be happening.

A thin man moved forward, studying the painting's gilt frame with gloved hands. "It's wired to an alarm."

Blue Eyes, clearly the group's leader, turned and aimed the gun at Gus' barrel chest. "Disconnect it."

"No," the guard said belligerently.

"I'm not asking."

Haven held up her hands. "Please—"

The gun fired. Gus dropped to one knee, pressing a hand to his shoulder.

"No!" she cried.

The leader stepped forward and pressed the gun to the older man's head.

"No." Haven fought back her fear and panic. "Don't hurt him. I'll disconnect it."

Slowly, she inched toward the painting, carefully avoiding the thin man still standing close to it. She touched the security panel built in beside the frame, pressing her palm to the small pad.

A second later, there was a discreet beep.

Two other men came forward and grabbed the frame.

She glanced around at them. "You're making a mistake. If you know who owns this museum, then you know you won't get away with this." Who would go up against the Norcross family? Easton, rich as sin, had a lot of connections, but his brother, Vander... Haven suppressed a shiver. Gia's middle brother might be hot, but he scared the bejesus out of Haven.

Vander Norcross, former military badass, owned Norcross Security and Investigations. His team had put in the high-tech security for the museum.

No one in their right mind wanted to go up against Vander, or the third Norcross brother who also worked with Vander, or the rest of Vander's team of badasses.

"Look, if you just—"

The blow to her head made her stagger. She blinked, pain radiating through her face. Blue Eyes had back-handed her.

He moved in and hit her again, and Haven cried out, clutching her face. It wasn't the first time she'd been hit. Her douchebag ex had hit her once. That was the day she'd left him for good.

But this was worse. Way worse.

"Shut up, you stupid bitch."

The next blow sent her to the floor. She thought she heard someone chuckle. He followed with a kick to her ribs, and Haven curled into a ball, a sob in her throat.

Her vision wavered and she blinked. Blue Eyes crouched down, putting his hand to the tiles right in front of her. Dizziness hit her, and she vaguely took in the freckles on the man's hand. They formed a spiral pattern.

"No one talks back to me," the man growled. "Especially a woman." He moved away.

She saw the men were busy maneuvering the painting off the wall. It was easy for two people to move.

She knew its exact dimensions—eighty by one hundred centimeters.

No one was paying any attention to her. Fighting through the nausea and dizziness, she dragged herself a few inches across the floor, closer to the nearby pillar. A pillar that had one of several hidden, high-tech panic buttons built into it.

When the men were turned away, she reached up and pressed the button.

Then blackness sucked her under.

HAVEN SAT on one of the lovely wooden benches she'd had installed around the museum. She'd wanted somewhere for guests to sit and take in the art.

She'd never expected to be sitting on one, holding a melting ice pack to her throbbing face, and staring at the empty wall where a multi-million-dollar masterpiece should be hanging. And she definitely didn't expect to be doing it with police dusting black powder all over the museum's walls.

Tears pricked her eyes. She was alive, her guards were hurt but alive, and that was what mattered. The police had questioned her and she'd told them everything she could remember. The paramedics had checked her over and given her the ice pack. Nothing was broken, but she'd been told to expect swelling and bruising.

David and Gus had been taken to the hospital. She'd been assured the men would be okay. Last she'd heard, David was in surgery. Her throat tightened. *Oh, God.*

What was she going to tell Easton?

Haven bit her lip and a tear fell down her cheek. She hadn't cried in months. She'd shed more than enough tears over Leo after he'd gone crazy and hit her. She'd left Miami the next day. She'd needed to get away from her ex and, unfortunately, despite loving her job at a classy Miami art gallery, Leo's cousin had owned it. Alyssa had been the one who had introduced them.

Haven had learned a painful lesson to not mix business and pleasure.

She'd been done with Leo's growing moodiness, outbursts, and cheating on her and hitting her had been the last straw. *Asshole.*

She wiped the tear away. San Francisco was as far from Miami as she could get and still be in the continental US. This was supposed to be her fresh new start.

She heard footsteps—solid, quick, and purposeful. Easton strode in.

He was a tall man, with dark hair that curled at the collar of his perfectly fitted suit. Haven had sworn off men, but she was still woman enough to appreciate her boss' good looks. His mother was Italian-American, and she'd passed down her very good genes to her children.

Like his brothers, Easton had been in the military, too, although he'd joined the Army Rangers. It showed in his muscled body. Once, she'd seen his shirt sleeves rolled up when they'd had a late meeting. He had some interesting ink that was totally at odds with his sophisticated-businessman persona.

His gaze swept the room, his jaw tight. It settled on her and he strode over.

"Haven—"

"Oh God, Easton. I'm so sorry."

He sat beside her and took her free hand. He squeezed her cold fingers, then he looked at her face and cursed.

She hadn't been brave enough to look in the mirror, but she guessed it was bad.

"They took the *Water Lilies*," she said.

"Okay, don't worry about it just now."

She gave a hiccupping laugh. "Don't worry? It's worth a hundred and ten *million* dollars."

A muscle ticked in his jaw. "You're okay, and that's the main thing. And the guards are in serious but stable condition at the hospital."

She nodded numbly. "It's all my fault."

Easton's gaze went to the police, and then moved back to her. "That's not true."

"I let them in." Her voice broke. God, she wanted the marble floor to crack and swallow her.

"Don't worry." Easton's face turned very serious. "Vander and Rhys will find the painting."

Her boss' tone made her shiver. Something made her suspect that Easton wanted his brothers to find the men who'd stolen the painting more than recovering the priceless piece of art.

She licked her lips, and felt the skin on her cheek tug. She'd have some spectacular bruises later. *Great. Thanks, universe.*

Then Easton's head jerked up, and Haven followed his gaze.

A man stood in the doorway. She hadn't heard him

coming. Nope, Vander Norcross moved silently, like a ghost.

He was a few inches over six feet, had a powerful body, and radiated authority. His suit didn't do much to tone down the sense that a predator had stalked into the room. While Easton was handsome, Vander wasn't. His face was too rugged, and while both he and Easton had blue eyes, Vander's were dark indigo, and as cold as the deepest ocean depths.

He didn't look happy. She fought back a shiver.

Then another man stepped up beside Vander.

Haven's chest locked. *Oh, no. No, no, no.*

She should have known. He was Vander's top investigator. Rhys Matteo Norcross, the youngest of the Norcross brothers.

At first glance, he looked like his brothers—similar build, muscular body, dark hair and bronze skin. But Rhys was the youngest, and he had a charming edge his brothers didn't share. He smiled more frequently, and his shaggy, thick hair always made her imagine him as a rock star, holding a guitar and making girls scream.

Haven was also totally, one hundred percent in lust with him. Any time he got near, he made her body flare to life, her heart beat faster, and made her brain freeze up. She could barely talk around the man.

She did *not* want Rhys Norcross to notice her. Or talk to her. Or turn his soulful, brown eyes her way.

Nuh-uh. No way. She'd sworn off men. This one should have a giant warning sign hanging on him. *Watch out, heartbreak waiting to happen.*

Rhys had been in the military with Vander. Some

hush-hush special unit that no one talked about. Now he worked at Norcross Security—apparently finding anything and anyone.

He also raced cars and boats in his free time. The man liked to go fast. Oh, and he bedded women. His reputation was legendary. Rhys liked a variety of adventures and experiences.

It was lucky Haven had sworn off men.

Especially when they happened to be her boss' brother.

And especially, especially when they were also her best friend's brother.

Off limits.

She saw the pair turn to look her and Easton's way.

Crap. Pulse racing, she looked at her bare feet and red toenails, which made her realize she hadn't recovered her shoes yet. They were her favorites.

She felt the men looking at her, and like she was drawn by a magnet, she looked up. Vander was scowling. Rhys' dark gaze was locked on her.

Haven's traitorous heart did a little tango in her chest.

Before she knew what was happening, Rhys went down on one knee in front of her.

She saw rage twist his handsome features. Then he shocked her by cupping her jaw, and pushing the ice pack away.

They'd never talked much. At Gia's parties, Haven purposely avoided him. He'd never touched her before, and she felt the warmth of him singe through her.

His eyes flashed. "It's going to be okay, baby."

Baby?

He stroked her cheekbone, those long fingers gentle.

Fighting for some control, Haven closed her hand over his wrist. She swallowed. "I—"

"Don't worry, Haven. I'm going to find the man who did this to you and make him regret it."

Her belly tightened. *Oh, God.* When was the last time anyone had looked out for her like this? She was certain no one had ever promised to hunt anyone down for her. Her gaze dropped to his lips.

He had amazingly shaped lips, a little fuller than such a tough man should have, framed by dark stubble.

There was a shift in his eyes and his face warmed. His fingers kept stroking her skin and she felt that caress all over.

Then she heard the click of heels moving at speed. Gia burst into the room.

"What the hell is going on?"

Haven jerked back from Rhys and his hypnotic touch. Damn, she'd been proven right—she was so weak where this man was concerned.

Gia hurried toward them. She was five-foot-four, with a curvy, little body, and a mass of dark, curly hair. As usual, she wore one of her power suits—short skirt, fitted jacket, and sky-high heels.

"Out of my way." Gia shouldered Rhys aside. When her friend got a look at Haven, her mouth twisted. "I'm going to *kill* them."

"Gia," Vander said. "The place is filled with cops. Maybe keep your plans for murder and vengeance quiet."

"Fix this." She pointed at Vander's chest, then at

Rhys. Then she turned and hugged Haven. "You're coming home with me."

"Gia—"

"No. No arguments." Gia held up her palm like a traffic cop. Haven had seen "the hand" before. It was pointless arguing.

Besides, she realized she didn't want to be alone. And the quicker she got away from Rhys' dark, far-too-perceptive gaze, the better.

Norcross Security

The Investigator
The Troubleshooter
The Specialist
The Bodyguard
The Hacker
The Powerbroker
The Detective
The Medic
The Protector
Also Available as Audiobooks!

PREVIEW: TREASURE HUNTER SECURITY

W ant to learn more about *Treasure Hunter Security*? Check out the first book in the series, *Undiscovered*, Declan Ward's action-packed story.

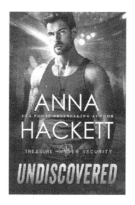

One former Navy SEAL. One dedicated archeologist. One secret map to a fabulous lost oasis.

Finding undiscovered treasures is always daring,

dangerous, and deadly. Perfect for the men of Treasure Hunter Security. Former Navy SEAL Declan Ward is haunted by the demons of his past and throws everything he has into his security business—Treasure Hunter Security. Dangerous archeological digs – no problem. Daring expeditions – sure thing. Museum security for invaluable exhibits – easy. But on a simple dig in the Egyptian desert, he collides with a stubborn, smart archeologist, Dr. Layne Rush, and together they get swept into a deadly treasure hunt for a mythical lost oasis. When an evil from his past reappears, Declan vows to do anything to protect Layne.

Dr. Layne Rush is dedicated to building a successful career—a promise to the parents she lost far too young. But when her dig is plagued by strange accidents, targeted by a lethal black market antiquities ring, and artifacts are stolen, she is forced to turn to Treasure Hunter Security, and to the tough, sexy, and too-used-to-giving-orders Declan. Soon her organized dig morphs into a wild treasure hunt across the desert dunes.

Danger is hunting them every step of the way, and Layne and Declan must find a way to work together...to not only find the treasure but to survive.

Treasure Hunter Security

Undiscovered

Uncharted

Unexplored

Unfathomed

Untraveled

Unmapped
Unidentified
Undetected
Also Available as Audiobooks!

ALSO BY ANNA HACKETT

Fury Brothers

Fury

Keep

Burn

Take

Claim

Also Available as Audiobooks!

Unbroken Heroes

The Hero She Needs

The Hero She Wants

The Hero She Craves

Also Available as Audiobooks!

Sentinel Security

Wolf

Hades

Striker

Steel

Excalibur

Hex

Stone

Also Available as Audiobooks!

Norcross Security

The Investigator

The Troubleshooter

The Specialist

The Bodyguard

The Hacker

The Powerbroker

The Detective

The Medic

The Protector

Mr. & Mrs. Norcross

Also Available as Audiobooks!

Billionaire Heists

Stealing from Mr. Rich

Blackmailing Mr. Bossman

Hacking Mr. CEO

Also Available as Audiobooks!

Team 52

Mission: Her Protection

Mission: Her Rescue

Mission: Her Security

Mission: Her Defense

Mission: Her Safety

Mission: Her Freedom

Mission: Her Shield

Mission: Her Justice

Also Available as Audiobooks!

Treasure Hunter Security

Undiscovered

Uncharted

Unexplored

Unfathomed

Untraveled

Unmapped

Unidentified

Undetected

Also Available as Audiobooks!

Oronis Knights

Knightmaster

Knighthunter

Galactic Kings

Overlord

Emperor

Captain of the Guard

Conqueror

Also Available as Audiobooks!

Eon Warriors

Edge of Eon

Touch of Eon

Heart of Eon

Kiss of Eon

Mark of Eon

Claim of Eon

Storm of Eon

Soul of Eon

King of Eon

Also Available as Audiobooks!

Galactic Gladiators: House of Rone

Sentinel

Defender

Centurion

Paladin

Guard

Weapons Master

Also Available as Audiobooks!

Galactic Gladiators

Gladiator

Warrior

Hero

Protector

Champion

Barbarian

Beast

Rogue

Guardian

Cyborg

Imperator

Hunter

Also Available as Audiobooks!

Hell Squad

Marcus

Cruz

Gabe

Reed

Roth

Noah

Shaw

Holmes

Niko

Finn

Devlin

Theron

Hemi

Ash

Levi

Manu

Griff

Dom

Survivors

Tane

Also Available as Audiobooks!

The Anomaly Series

Time Thief

Mind Raider

Soul Stealer

Salvation

Anomaly Series Box Set

The Phoenix Adventures

Among Galactic Ruins

At Star's End

In the Devil's Nebula

On a Rogue Planet

Beneath a Trojan Moon

Beyond Galaxy's Edge

On a Cyborg Planet

Return to Dark Earth

On a Barbarian World

Lost in Barbarian Space

Through Uncharted Space

Crashed on an Ice World

Perma Series

Winter Fusion

A Galactic Holiday

Warriors of the Wind

Tempest

Storm & Seduction

Fury & Darkness

Standalone Titles

Savage Dragon

Hunter's Surrender

One Night with the Wolf

For more information visit www.annahackett.com

ABOUT THE AUTHOR

I'm a USA Today bestselling romance author who's passionate about **_fast-paced, emotion-filled_** contemporary romantic suspense and science fiction romance. I love writing about people overcoming unbeatable odds and achieving seemingly impossible goals. I like to believe it's possible for all of us to do the same.

I live in Australia with my own personal hero and two very busy, always-on-the-move sons.

For release dates, behind-the-scenes info, free books, and other fun stuff, sign up for the latest news here:

Website: www.annahackett.com

Made in United States
Troutdale, OR
12/10/2024

26227622R00154